MURDER
TO
MIL-SPEC

An anthology to benefit
Homes for Our Troops

To Denise
A true fan —
Thanks for letting
me use your
name!
All best,
Bob

Wolfmont

MURDER TO MIL-SPEC
An anthology to benefit Homes for Our Troops

ISBN-13 978-1-60364-028-2

For information, contact:
info@wolfmont.com
or
Wolfmont Press
238 Park Drive NE
Ranger, GA 30734

Table of Contents

Foreword

When I was younger (much younger) I was a military man. I joined at the tail end of the Viet Nam conflict—spent over twelve years in the U.S. Navy, and about eighteen months in the Army National Guard. I saw some terrible injuries happen to people, but the current conflicts in Iraq, Afghanistan, and other places far to the east of our comfortable homes in the U.S. have ushered in a new wave of horrors.

The use of IEDs and homicide bombers by insurgents and others in these places has created a massive new problem for the military: soldiers who survive, but who are so badly injured that normal housing just won't work for them.

I won't say "handicapped" or "disabled," because these men and women who come through such horrifying attacks display extraordinary able-ness: the ability to survive, the ability to cope, the ability to learn new ways to do things, the ability to accept that some obstacles exist, and then develop ways to go around, over or through those obstacles. It is, I believe, a necessary component of the psyche of any military person. Clint Eastwood expressed it best in one of my favorite movies, *Heartbreak Ridge* —the ability to "Improvise, adapt, and overcome."

Even with that ability, however, comes the

realization that sometimes help is needed. And that help is where organizations like **Homes for Our Troops** really stand out. Since 2004, Homes for Our Troops has built 62 homes for returning veterans, at no cost to the veteran, and there are usually about 40 under construction at any given time.

There is not room in this book to tell you all about what Homes for Our Troops accomplishes to help those veterans who return home and need a place to live that is accessible and livable. Because of that, I invite you to check them out on the web at www.homesforourtroops.org . I promise you, you will be touched, and uplifted, by what this organization is doing.

That is why this book was published to benefit Homes for Our Troops. The work they do is vital. These men and women—veterans who return with missing limbs or without the ability to do certain things—need our help, and I can't think of a finer cause to support.

The authors and I hope you will agree.

Tony Burton
Editor

Meet Me by the Priest

Terrie Farley Moran

The same week the Allies reached the outskirts of Berlin, my outfit left the South Pacific, heading stateside on rotation. We'd spent more than three years hop-scotching around the nameless islands scattered between New Zealand and nowhere. We broke our backs clearing land, unpacking supplies and setting up bases. Holding ground.

The Germans were down for the count in Europe. The Japanese were dug in on Okinawa but we were pounding them day and night. Rumors of their complete surrender raged through our transport, but in our hearts, we knew wishful thinking when we heard it.

We landed in Norfolk. Our Captain and some First Sergeant from the MPs gave us an unholy sermon—a long list of do's and don'ts—before we got our passes with orders to report to some camp down south by 0600 thirty-one days out.

I jumped on a Greyhound, changed in D.C. and hit New York just before dawn. The bus terminal on Thirty-fourth Street was mobbed with uniforms and a sprinkling of civilians. During my time overseas, hemlines had shortened. I enjoyed watching young, shapely gams perched on high heels click their way across the waiting room. To discourage unnecessary travel, posters of a grandmotherly type were plastered on the dingy terminal walls. Her heartrending smile pleaded, "Stay home to bring our boys home."

After my mother died in '43, my father kept the apartment on Thirty-ninth Street. My Aunt Molly wrote that the old man was more at home on a barstool in Kealey's over on Second Avenue, but at least I'd have a bed and a place to change into civvies. A lot of guys would come home to less.

I shouldered my duffle and headed east.

Streaks of early morning sun slithered through the overhead tracks of the Third Avenue El. The rumbling of the downtown IRT train welcomed me. I made a left and followed the tracks towards home. Near the corner of Thirty-seventh Street, a voice came from the shadows.

"Is that the Scully champion of Thirty-ninth Street? Good you're back, Corporal Billy."

A match struck the El pillar. The glow brightened as Tawny inhaled the flame to light his cigarette. As kids we stole loosies from the candy store. He always grabbed the Old Golds. I wondered if that was still his smoke.

I dropped my duffle. We shook hands and examined each other's faces for signs of what the war might have done.

"What are you doing home? Finished with Uncle Sam?"

"Nah. Been rock hoppin' for so long that our rotation number came up. I head back in a month. You? How'd you get out of Australia?"

"An unfortunate incident with an officer's wife." Tawny shrugged. "You know how it is."

"Should've known. Trouble and babes are all the same with you. How come you're not in Leavenworth?"

"The officer has career plans and needed me to go away quietly. I held out for Fort Hamilton. I got no real job there, so most nights I catch the D train from Bensonhurst and here I am."

"Your officer must have some juice to get you transferred to Brooklyn."

"He's a two star, hoping the war'll last long

enough to make him a three star."

"A general! You couldn't keep your hands off a general's wife?"

"Hey, she got me home ahead of you, Goody Two Shoes. Besides she was carrying a real heavy torch for me." There went that shrug again. "Come on, the after-hours joints are still open. I'll buy you a beer."

"Nah, first thing, see the old man."

Tawny flicked his cigarette into the middle of the street. "Yeah, okay, but catch up with me later. There's a ginmill I want to try up on Forty-eighth just off Ninth. Them westside broads can't wait to meet us."

"Since when do we drink on the Westside? I ain't lookin' for a fight."

"The war changed everything. The East-West battles are long over. Meet me in the Cavan Rose. Anytime after nine. Wear your uniform. Dames are khaki wacky these days."

***

My father turned on the oven to toast some bread and set a pot on the stovetop to boil water for tea. Once we sat he fell silent, his hands worrying the edge of the grimy oilcloth covering the table.

"Shame about your mother."

I agreed.

"Your Aunt Molly will be wanting you to supper."

Then he pulled his cap off the hook by the door, muttered something about errands and fled to Kealeys.

The cramped parlor hadn't changed. The battered Philco radio still sat atop a wobbly mahogany table. I sat in the oldest of the three chairs, once dark green, long faded to a murky gray. Even now I could feel my brothers squishing me in the middle of the chair as we all squealed with terror, sometimes covering our ears, but never once missing the adventures of The Shadow. Tim's in Italy. He'd be home soon, but Joe's outfit was pushing a lot further north in the Pacific than I'd ever been.

***

Sitting center bar at the Cavan Rose, Tawny was surrounded by nearly a dozen sailors wearing a uniform I didn't recognize.

"Here he is, boyos. My best buddy since we were five, and will be until we're fifty, God bless we make it." Nods of agreement all around, with a few "sure you will's" thrown in.

"This is Billy Shane." Tawny reached behind my head and pulled me into the circle.

"Billy, let me introduce the whole Royal Canadian Navy."

"If not the entire, certainly the best of it. I'm Gil." said a brawny sailor, whose face had the beat up look of an experienced fighter. He insisted on buying my "catch up" drink. The party had been moving along without me.

One sailor, who stood no higher than my chin, was called "Schnoz," in honor of the Jimmy Durante nose he sported. He pulled a Canadian quarter from behind my right ear, declared it useless in New York and found an American quarter behind my left. One minute he'd be with us laughing and talking, the next he was dragging a string of colored hankies out of the sleeve of a rum-dumb at the end of the bar.

One drink led to another. The sailors' shore leave was dwindling, so Tawny invited them to meet us the next night on the Westside at O'Looney's.

"Can't miss it. Just up the block from Madison Square Garden. And don't forget to visit the priest on your way."

For his finale, Schnoz moseyed over to three old ladies sipping wine at a corner table. He pulled a bouquet of paper flowers from under the worn velvet hat of the woman who looked to be the oldest, presented it to her with a flourish, and the Canadians were out the door.

I bought one last round. "Why a Westside bar? Westsiders don't like Eastside guys any more than we like them. Let's stay on our own side of Fifth."

"We already know all the broads on the east side, but on the west side there are fresh farms to be plowed, if you catch my meaning."

He was too soused for any argument, so I changed the subject. "Why are you sending the Canadians to a priest? They Catholic?"

"Not a priest. The priest. Father Duffy."

"You mean the statue?"

"I do, indeed. Father Duffy of the old Fighting 69th is a good luck charm for us grunts. The Mirror had a story about how this Canadian priest became an American Army hero during the Great War."

"Canadian?"

Born there. Came here. That's why I told Gil and the boyos to say a prayer at the statue. He'll take care of 'em. And he's right there on Forty-seventh and Broadway, a stones throw from O'Looney's."

***

I spent the next afternoon visiting my

mother's friends, the ones who helped during her last days while my brothers and I were far away. I thanked them for their kindness to her and each one cried as she spoke of Ma's bravery at the end.

Just around suppertime, the doorbell rang. It was a kid, about eleven, looked familiar. I probably played stickball with his older brother years ago.

"Telephone call at the candy store for Corporal Billy. That you?"

No need to ask who was calling. I gave the kid a nickel and sent him off to say I'd be right there.

"A gorgeous dolly I been asking out, finally said yes. A redhead. Works in Macy's. I love redheads. Anyway she's meeting us at O'Looney's. Eight o'clock. Bringing a friend for you, so now we got no choice. Some old guy said it. 'Go west, young man.'"

It was easier to give in. I could argue but eventually he'd have us drinking on the westside. Probably brawling, too. I figured there was less chance of trouble if we showed up with our own girls.

We walked across Forty-third and I stopped at St. Agnes to light a candle for my brothers. Then we zigged and zagged until we were at the north end of Times Square, Forty-seventh and Broadway.

There he was, Father Duffy, towering above us. People had strewn flowers all over the sidewalk and along the base of his pedestal. The stone Celtic Cross behind him had pictures and notes taped front and back. Two Marines were standing at attention directly in front of the priest. One leaned in and touched the Bible in Father Duffy's hands.

Tawny elbowed me as we crossed Broadway. "What'd I tell ya? It's like he's a saint or somethin'."

The saloon smell of beer and tobacco was softened by the scent of second-rate perfumes. I set my elbow down on the bar, ordered two beers, and swiveled my bar stool to get a good look at O'Looney's.

She stood in the doorway in a short, tight dress, the blue-green color of the Pacific at dawn. A fresh white gardenia caught her auburn curls behind a dainty ear. I swear there was a quick hush before the talk picked up again.

Out of the side of his mouth, Tawny asked, "What do ya think?" and waved her over.

A less flashy brunette trailed behind. That

was the one I thought would do.

Introductions all around. I gave Angie, the brunette, my seat and watched as the redhead snuggled into Tawny's side like the wedding was tomorrow. Tawny signaled the bartender, who dragged his feet getting over to us.

The redhead leaned in and said, "I'll have the usual, Mike."

"Jeez, Linda," the bartender whined. "What a you doin'? O'Looney'll be here any minute. He'll kill you. You too, soldier. Get out now."

The bartender's word is always law. I was reaching for the fiver I'd dropped on the bar, when the redhead waggled a finger in the barkeep's face.

"Jack O'Looney threw me out on my keister like Friday's fish bones. He don't have nothing to say. Pour our drinks."

Tawny backed her up. "You heard the lady," even though we all knew this Linda was no lady.

The bartender wiped his hands on his apron and muttered, "Your funeral," before he went off to fill our order.

Angie was quick to tell me that she worked with Linda but had never been out with her before.

Silence, sudden and absolute, was the tipoff.

He was standing just behind Tawny's bar stool. A sharp-chinned guy, mid-thirties, snappy dresser in a gray suit with a matching fedora he hadn't bothered to remove when he came indoors. A couple of pug-uglies flanked him.

Tawny was asking Linda if she wanted to hop a cab to Sammys on the Bowery. He seemed not to notice the place had gone quiet.

The barman cleared his throat. "Mr. O'Looney, care to wet your whistle?"

Linda threw a satisfied smile at O'Looney and began to rub circles on Tawny's uniform shirt.

O'Looney ignored her and looked straight at Tawny.

"Haven't seen you in my place before." He took out a silver cigarette case and pushed it past Linda to offer a Bond Street to Tawny, who took a pass.

One of the pug-uglies whipped out a lighter. While blazing O'Looney's cigarette, he managed to elbow Linda. Her objection was shrill, her language salty. She threw a challenging look at Tawny, who slid from his bar stool.

"Soldier, why not just leave the dame to me? I promise she isn't worth the trouble."

Linda wouldn't shut up. "You want trouble, I'll tell your sloppy wife about us. Better yet, I'll talk to the cops. A girl hears a lot when she's around you."

Tawny thrust himself between Linda and O'Looney. I closed ranks, standing shoulder to shoulder with him.

"We feared you fellas forgot about our last night on the town." Schnoz appeared in the small space between Tawny and O'Looney. "Hello, and what have we here?" He pulled a quarter from behind the ear of the pug-ugly in the brown suit. "Lose this, champ?"

O'Looney lifted a hand as if to swat Schnoz away like an annoying fly but Gil reached in and grabbed his wrist. "Not a good idea, pal. He don't like to be shoved around."

O'Looney saw that the bar was overflowing with sailors, and took a step back.

"Your day'll come, soldier."

"Linda." His glare and a quick flap of his hand ordered her to leave.

She wrapped her arms around Tawny and gave him a kiss filled with promises. "Tomorrow night. Sammy's. Come on, Angie." And she walked slowly to the door, aware that every man in the joint was watching her go.

O'Looney and his muscle disappeared through a door beside the jukebox. I suggested that our crew wander up the block and try to get into Jack Dempsey's restaurant on Broadway.

Gil hoped out loud that The Champ was signing autographs and maybe buying drinks for Allies shipping out the next day.

I dragged Tawny along, knowing he was thinking something dumb.

As it turned out, Jack Dempsey's stint in the U.S. Coast Guard gave him a history with Canadian sailors. He liked our bunch from the start and treated all of us like long lost cronies. Schnoz worked his magic tricks on a few high rollers at the bar. He finished by lifting Dempsey's wallet and returning it. The Champ feigned an uppercut to Schnoz's jaw for the house camera and signed the print.

We closed the place and walked down Broadway in high spirits, exchanging addresses and offering Schnoz outrageous sums of money for his Dempsey picture. We ended with a somber moment visiting Father Duffy.

Schnoz pulled me aside. "Been fun hanging out with you Yankee fellas. Your cranky friend will do some penance looking for this, I suppose. Serves him right." And he handed me one of his colorful hankies wrapped around a silver cigarette case. I flipped the cloth and read the engraving: John F. O'Looney.

I stuffed it into my pocket and gave the wily imp a bear hug.

The sailors wished us Godspeed and piled into a couple of oversized checker cabs.

Tawny and I walked back toward Thirty-ninth Street.

"This Linda babe is my last chance."

I scoffed. "There are plenty of broads. Tomorrow we'll hit the east Fifties."

"Some jerk at Fort Hamilton figured out that I'm stationed there with no job, no nothing. So they cut my orders for Adak in the Aleutian Islands. I had to find it on a map. Bunch of rocks off Alaska. The Japanese attacked the Aleutians early in the war. Army's afraid they might try again to distract us from Okinawa. My orders are already cut."

"When?"

"Thursday. I only got tomorrow and Wednesday. I know you're going to tell me to stay away from Sammys tomorrow night. Just let her go. But I can't. I don't have time to find another dolly."

So there we were Tuesday night sitting at a ringside table in Sammys. Linda, her red hair piled high and held in place with tiger-eye combs, was giving Tawny all the right signals. Being the fifth wheel, I pretended to watch the show but mostly I kept my eye on the crowd for any sign of O'Looney or his goons.

The lovebirds were eager to be alone so, at the end of the band's first set, we hailed a cab. They dropped me on Thirty-ninth Street. I stopped by Kealey's to have a night cap with my father, but he and a couple of other old'uns were deep in deciding what to do with Hitler when they found him. I had a quick beer then walked home to find my bed.

***

Someone poked my shoulder. I leaped out of bed, afraid I missed Reveille. My father said, "The Romano kid come by. You got a phone call at the candy store. I said you'd be right there. Wasn't for the morning papers, nobody'd be there to answer."

"Jeez, dad, did you have to wake me?"

"Watch your mouth in this house." And he closed the bedroom door.

I pulled on the crumpled pants lying on the

floor, grabbed my shirt from the door knob and scarcely stopped to tie my shoes.

I could hardly make out the whisper.

"Meet me by the priest."

"Tawny?"

"Meet me." And the line went dead.

I found him on the Broadway side of the statue, sitting on the curb, his head cradled in his hands.

"I'm done for. She's dead."

"Ease up. Who's dead?"

"I woke up. Linda was dead. Pillow on the floor, smeared with makeup, like some one held it over her face, but there was no one there except me and her."

I tugged his arm until he stood.

"Come on, lets get some coffee and you can prove to me you're not bats."

"You didn't ask if I killed her."

"You didn't. You hardly knew her, and you were sober when you dropped me. A drunken rampage is the only thing that would get you murderous. And I've only seen you that drunk once.

"Dumpheys wedding. Jackass doctored the whiskey with hooch. Same thing happened when I bought a bottle of gin from some guy had a still

18

on Tarawa. Made me too sick to do anything but wish I was dead, when I wasn't trying to kill the guy who made the gin."

If you had enough nickels for the coin slots, you could get a ten course meal in the Automat on Forty-second Street. I pushed nickels in a slot and got us two cups of coffee. I kept his black. He ignored the steam rising from his cup and drained it dry. My tongue burned from watching. I got him another coffee, this time adding milk.

Halfway through his second cup, Tawny cast an eye on the nearby tables to make sure he couldn't be overheard.

"We had a swell time. She was fun. You know."

I could guess.

"We had our last tumble around three, then fell asleep. I woke up a couple of hours later and she was dead."

"Where . . . ?"

"Short sheet place on west Forty-fifth."

"Room in your name?"

"I waited on the sidewalk. When she waved me in, we had a big laugh. Seems she registered as Mr. and Mrs. John Francis O'Looney. Kept saying it would have been even better if she could figure a way to make him pay the freight."

"You sure she's dead?"

He grimaced.

Stupid question. He'd seen plenty of death. We both had.

"Still got the room key?"

He squirmed and pulled it from his pocket. I grabbed it.

"Did you leave anything in the room? Wallet? Papers? Clothes?"

"Only had the clothes on my back. It was a one nighter, so I made sure nothing left my pockets. Some of these girls'll roll a guy." His sheepish half smile told me I wasn't the only Eastside guy got caught in that trap. I knew Tawny was no killer, still I checked the booze angle again.

"You buy a bottle?"

"Nah. She was in a big hurry to get to the room. Me, too. Oh, God. My life ain't worth a plugged nickel. Might as well call the cops now."

"Not yet. You stay here." I stood up, patted my pockets, then I dropped a handful of nickels in front of his coffee cup. "Have some breakfast. Don't move from this table."

As I walked to Forty-fifth Street, the last few days kept spinning through my mind. Okay, Tawny meets the redhead. Was she the one put

20

O'Looney's in his mind? Probably. We get there and find out she's the sometime girlfriend of O'Looney, who's not the cleanest guy around. Linda can't keep her mouth shut and threatens to blab to O'Looney's wife and the coppers besides. The puzzle wasn't hard to complete. O'Looney knew we were going to Sammy's last night. He follows along and when Tawny and Linda were asleep, O'Looney knocked off Linda and left Tawny for the patsy.

The hotel lobby was deserted. I stood outside, trying to look casual, until I heard the telephone ring. When the desk clerk answered it, I slipped past and ran up the stairs. I let myself into room 306.

Linda was dead, okay. I gave the room a quick once over. No way to tell who'd been here with the girl. Not a sign of Tawny. One thing the Army taught us. Keep your stuff tight, ready to move. Good he followed that rule.

Registration was for Mister and Missus, but no one would be surprised if it turned out to be Mister and his bimbo. I could seal that deal. I took O'Looney's cigarette case wrapped in Schnoz's red handkerchief out of my pocket and stepped into the bathroom. I wedged the case on the floor between the sink and the toilet, right where it would fall out of a guy's pocket when he was sitting on the throne.

I kept the hanky for good luck.

Back downstairs, two girls were arguing about their phone bill with the desk clerk. I blew right by.

Tawny was off the hook for Linda's murder. He could ship out to the Aleutians without looking over his shoulder, and, God willing, in a few months we'd all be home for good.

Dart Champ

Dorothy Francis

Agnes Brown opened the bottom drawer of her jewelry box and reached for her gold ring.

Gone!

She shuffled and reshuffled the drawer contests, to no avail. Gone. Her replica of the Bronze Star she'd received for meritorious service during WWII, gone! A glance told her the original award still hung in its ebony frame above her writing desk across the room.

She knew exactly where she always kept the ring. She might be eighty-five, but her memory was as razor sharp now as it had been in France in 1944 when she field-tested walkie-talkies in Normandy. Any member at the Senior Center could vouch for her memory.

She played winning bridge at the center every Tuesday, and on Thursdays she challenged all contenders as she defended her Dart Champ title. Why, a reporter featured her in the local newspaper when she defeated former champ,

Deadeye Dixon. A person with a flawed memory couldn't perform as perfectly and consistently as she did.

Nobody had access to her bedroom suite and jewelry box except her housekeeper, Roxie. Now Agnes searched for tactful words to use in questioning the woman about the ring as Roxie began dusting the marble top dressing table.

"No, Mrs. Brown, I ain't seen nothing of your ring," Roxie paused as she brushed bottle-blonde bangs from her eyes. Then she dusted the intricate curlicues on the hand-carved walnut bedstead before she spoke again. "Of course, I never open your jewelry box. What's the ring look like?"

"The mounting is in burnished gold—large, heavy, oval shaped. Twenty-one carat." Agnes looked Roxie in the eye. "In the ring's center, a replica bronze star is fashioned in darker gold."

"The ring sounds mighty purty." Roxie began dusting the walnut night stand. "I think you've put it somewhere and forgotten where. Have you looked in the bathroom and the kitchen? Perhaps you shucked it off while you washed your hands."

"No," Agnes said. "I seldom wore the ring, and I promised it to my granddaughter on her twenty-first birthday. Gwen's coming soon and I planned to give it to her after I make my demonstration appearance at your husband's bar."

"The Brass Monkey? A lady like you gonna go there?"

"Yes. Not that I want to." Agnes felt her face flush at the thought of going into any bar— especially a bar on Sinclair Street. "Your husband has promised me a hundred dollars to give a thirty-minute dart-throwing demonstration for his patrons. I figured you knew about that."

"Sounds like easy bread to me," Roxie said. "A hundred bucks for thirty minutes of work. Wow! I'd like a piece of that action. Didn't know Jacko could be so generous."

"I'm certainly not accepting the money for myself," Agnes said. "I'm donating it to the Senior Center for their lift-chair fund. That's the only reason I'm doing the demonstration —want to help get the fund off to a good start. "

"Way cool, Mrs. Brown. But watch your back. That's a dangerous part of town— especially after dark."

"I'm not worried about my back," Agnes said. "Gwen's a policewoman. She's promised to take care of both of us—not that we're expecting any trouble."

Roxie shook her head. "I'll keep an eye out for your ring as I clean. It's gotta be somewhere in the house."

"Maybe so," Agnes said. She knew she hadn't mislaid the ring, but she knew she couldn't come right out and accuse Roxie of stealing it. She had no evidence of that. It would be her word against Roxie's. But she thought of one thing she could do.

As soon as Roxie left for the day, Agnes drove to her insurance company and approached the clerk sitting at her computer in the outer office.

"Miss Rankin, I'd like to report my gold ring stolen. You know the one. The bronze star replica. I've carried insurance on it with this company for years."

"Yes," Miss Rankin said. "I remember the ring. But you'll have to report your loss to the police before we can make payment." She searched her files and pulled out a picture of the missing ring. "Take this picture with you, Mrs. Brown. Maybe the police will find it useful in finding or identifying your property."

"I hope someone can find it," Agnes said. "I

know my granddaughter would much rather have a keepsake ring than the insurance money."

Agnes picked up the picture, thanked the clerk, and headed for the police station.

Tobacco juice brown. That was the color of everything inside the station—walls, floor tile, furniture. Agnes almost choked on the stale smoke odor.

"May I help you, Ma'am?" an officer asked.

"I want to report a missing gold ring." Agnes pulled the picture from her purse, ready to tell the circumstances of her loss. But before she could get fully into her story, another officer stormed into the room.

"A Blake Buxton nude's been stolen from the art gallery," the officer announced. "One of Buxton's latest oils. The gallery's been closed a month for repairs. The painting could have been taken weeks ago. Buxton just now learned it was gone."

Agnes cleared her throat and the intruding officer stopped talking, clearly surprised at her presence. The officer who had been studying the ring picture rose, apologized for the intrusion, and quickly ushered Agnes from the room.

"I'll circulate this picture, Mrs. Brown. I hope we can get the ring back for you. If not, we'll let your insurance company know. You should have no trouble collecting your insurance money."

"Thank you," Agnes muttered, suspecting that her ring would be of low importance on the police blotter of missing objects. Blake Buxton, famous artist, would outrank Agnes Brown, elderly dart champ, in the eyes of the police. She sighed and drove back home.

The next evening when Gwen arrived, Agnes gave her a kiss then paused for a moment looking at her. Red hair. Creamy complexion. Slender build. Gwen looked a lot like Agnes had looked in her youth. Then, biting back tears of anger and frustration, she told Gwen about the stolen ring.

"I've looked everywhere for it, Gwen. It was to be yours. Years ago In the WAACs, I gave up a promotion for the privilege of serving my country overseas. My assignment involved field-testing walkie-talkies in Normandy shortly after D-day. Later, the Army awarded me the Bronze Star. In my will I've directed that the actual medal is be buried with me. But the replica ring was to be yours.

"Now it's gone. I've not accused Roxie, but I've dismissed her. Told her I decided to do the housework myself."

"Oh, Gram. How sad for you to lose your special ring—and to a thief!"

"Your ring, Gwen. Your ring. Yes, it's sad, but I want you to have the insurance money. That's a promise, and the ring's well insured."

"Maybe it will turn up." Gwen said. "Let's don't give up of finding it."

"All right, but now we must hurry to The Brass Monkey. I'm so glad you're here. I 'd be afraid to go into that neighborhood alone."

"Well, I'm not afraid," Gwen said, "and my police training has prepared me for emergencies," Gwen opened the car door for her grandmother and helped her inside.

"The crowd may be a bunch of toughs, but my appearance has been well advertised. Jacko Jackson wouldn't dare let anything bad happen at his bar tonight."

"Right," Gwen said. "Gram, how did you get to be so good at throwing darts?"

Agnes chuckled. "Practiced at USO centers during the war, Gwen. Lots of soldiers there were eager to help a lady any way they could. Tonight I'll give my demonstration, collect my money, and we'll leave."

Once in the car, Gwen drove for several

minutes through wide, well-lighted residential streets before they reached an area of low-income housing projects. Here, the streets were narrow and streetlights were few. Agnes remembered reading about vandals shooting out the bulbs with pellet guns. Luckily, they found a parking place near the front entrance of The Brass Monkey where gold neon against a flyspecked window outlined the shape of a long-tailed primate.

Once inside the bar, it took several minutes for Agnes's eyes to adjust to the dimness. The smell of cigar smoke all but sickened her. Jacko Jackson approached them, his beer-barrel belly leading the way. Wiping ham-like hands on his booze-stained bar apron, he led Agnes and Gwen to a table and motioned them to be seated.

"I'll stand if you don't mind." Agnes turned her back on the grease-stained chair Jacko offered as she placed her leather-bound dart case on the table and opened it. She tried to ignore the men who crowded around, peering at her, leering at Gwen, and also trying to sneak a close look at her darts.

"Whaddaya want to drink?" Jacko asked.

"Lemonade, please," Agnes said.

"Make it two," Gwen said when he looked at her.

"Comin' right up."

Agnes ignored the laughter of the bar patrons. "Where is the target, Sir?" she asked Jacko.

"To your left." Jacko pointed. Then he tapped the floor with his toe. "Please stand behind this white line. It's where the guys hafta stand. It's regulation for The Brass Monkey."

Agnes looked at the target. Narrow black circles of diminishing circumference ringed the scarlet bull's eye. It took Agnes a few moments to realize that the background for the target was a picture—a nude woman with a voluptuous body but indistinct facial features. Naturally, men would like that sort of target background. Who cared about facial features? Agnes pretended she had noticed nothing but the bull's eye. Then suddenly all her senses came alert. Her heart pounded. She could hardly swallow.

"May I examine that bull's eye?" she asked.

"Sure," Jacko replied. "Don't worry. It's on the up and up—strictly regulation size. You can measure it if you want to haggle about details."

Agnes approached the target slowly, her gaze skimming over the bull's eye. There on the nude's finger was an exact likeness of her unique ring. How could this be? She had to know the why and how of this.

She turned to Jacko. "May I make a quick private telephone call, please?" Agnes pulled her cell phone from her purse. "I've forgotten an important detail. Gwen, please stay here and keep an eye on my darts."

Jacko led Agnes to a private corner. "I hope this won't hold up the show. I haven't had a crowd like this in here for weeks. The guys could get nasty if there's too much of a wait."

"I'll be quick," Agnes promised.

Jacko strode away and Agnes dialed 911, stated her business, and returned to her dart case. She nodded to Jacko indicating that she was ready to begin her demonstration. Silence fell over the room as she threw a few warm-up shots.

The crowd of men and women fell back, giving her room as she stepped behind the white line. Her first dart hit the bull's eye. Amid applause and whistles, Agnes made a big thing of wiping her hands on a towel and examining the next dart carefully before she made her second throw.

Another bull's eye. And a third. And a fourth. Now her audience began to stamp their feet and shout, urging her on. There was too much noise for her to hear any sounds from outside. As she scored her tenth bull's eye, the front door of the saloon burst open and two burly policemen strode in with guns at the ready.

"Clear the bar, please," an officer ordered. "Everyone outside except the owner and the Browns."

At the sight of the police, the men left quietly. When they were gone, an officer carefully examined the painting before he approached Jacko with handcuffs.

"We're taking you and the Blake Buxton picture, the nude, downtown for questioning."

Jacko's eyed the exit and took a step toward it before his shoulders slumped. "How did you know?"

"Agnes Brown called us to report that she had a lead on her missing ring," the officer said. "Blake Buxton happens to be a close friend of mine and I recognize his work. How does the likeness of Mrs. Brown's gold ring happen to be on the finger of the model in the painting that's clearly Blake Buxton's missing oil? You have the right to call a lawyer before you answer."

"Don't want a lawyer," Jacko said. "My wife Roxie had been wearing that ring for weeks," Jacko said. "Then when she dragged me to an art show, I happened to notice her ring on the nude.

That's when I knew Roxie had posed for Buxton's painting. And I guessed who she'd been sleeping with on all those nights she told me she was taking art lessons.

Stealing the painting and using it as a target was part of my revenge. The other part was kicking Roxie out of my house." Jacko chuckled. "I hear Roxie has had to take up housecleaning to support herself. But she had the ring for weeks while the pic was being painted."

"Where's my ring right now?" Agnes demanded, stepping forward.

"Roxie has it," the officer said. "A backup man located her and is picking her up and bringing her to the station. Mrs. Brown, you're a smart detective to have figured this out. You'll get your ring back as well as the reward Buxton's offering for the painting."

"Give the reward to the Senior Center." Agnes watched the officer snap the cuffs on Jacko. "All I want is the pay for my demonstration and my ring to pass along to my granddaughter!"

Agnes took Gwen's arm as they left the bar and returned home.

Tripwire

Big Jim Williams

I sat in my car and stared at the heavy gun in my lap—a .44 Magnum—one of the deadliest handguns in the world. I had stolen it from Rongo Layton. How, wasn't important. But the plan I had for it was. I'd sawed its long barrel to a snub-nose two inches to create enough noise to bring neighbors and police. A white handkerchief circled the pistol's grips.

The irony: Rongo Layton couldn't report it stolen, because felons can't own guns.

I sat in the cool darkness for almost three hours. It was 1:30 in the morning, but somehow I stayed awake, parked under a long row of dark trees. My working halfway through a bottle of whiskey hadn't helped. I rubbed the old wounds on my stiff right leg. And there were the headaches, always the headaches. I would have waited forever if it meant the death of Lt. Rongo Layton.

I lowered my head as a car sped down the

main road, twisted into the narrow side street, hit the curb, and braked behind a two-story Colonial in one of Atlanta's upscale areas. The garage door rolled up. The black sports car slipped inside. The driver staggered from the vehicle, his lanky frame silhouetted against the garage's faint interior light. He was smoking a big corncob pipe.

It was Layton.

I hated that arrogant bastard. When I tell you why, maybe you'll understand.

***

I had met Layton years before. We had served together in the early '50s during the outbreak of the Korean War. He commanded Bravo Company. In the first weeks of that "police action" we spent more time running than fighting.

HQ scraped up every available dogface and Marine from Japan and the Pacific to help stop the mass of bugle-blowing Communist Chinese streaming south across the Yalu River. I hadn't been that frightened and tired since fighting in France in 1943. I hated being back in the Army. I had seen too much bloodshed. I was getting too old for this crap.

Rongo Layton wore lieutenant's bars and

strutted with an arrogance that General George S. Patton would have envied. He was a wet-nosed, ninety-day wonder looking for glory. He had more ambition than brains and a know-it-all attitude that produced dead soldiers—ours, not their's.

As a recycled World War II infantry Corporal, I came with a Purple Heart, eighteen months of European combat, and enough smarts to keep my head down, my GI-mouth shut, and to never volunteer.

Lt. Rongo Layton came with a need to see anyone's ass shot off if it meant his promotion. He was tall and handsome and bragged about his alleged sexual conquests. He claimed to be the nephew of the chairman of the U.S. Senate's powerful Military Appropriations Committee.

After WWII I'd joined the Army Reserves for weekend-warrior pay, but was suddenly activated when North Korea invaded South Korea in June of 1950.

I left behind a business that went belly-up, and Catherine, my beautiful blonde bride of six months. Losing my business hurt, but leaving Catherine left an emptiness that couldn't be filled.

North Korea quickly overran most of the

south. Then in September, General Douglas MacArthur made a surprise amphibious landing of American troops on South Korea's northwest coast. We fought through North Korea toward the Chinese border. But by December, a half million Chinese troops surged across the Yalu River to help unify Korea under the red banner of communism. U.S. and Southern Korean forces skedaddled south.

Our Bravo Company dug in a few miles below the 38th parallel.

Lt. Layton's clean hands soon gripped my transfer request. It wouldn't be my last. I respected good officers. He wasn't one. Two weeks earlier he'd replaced Capt. Warner Edwards, killed when his jeep hit a land mine.

A big MacArthur-style corncob occupied Layton's tight mouth. The tobacco was pungent. He idolized the general who successfully guided U.S. forces against Japan in World War II, and now led UN troops in Korea. Layton even wore MacArthur's famous sunglasses.

A framed copy of his BS degree from an obscure college hung on a sandbag behind his desk. I was to learn the BS stood for bullshit.

He looked like someone miscast in a high school play.

"Cpl. Clooney," he said, waving my transfer. "I don't like your attitude."

"Every soldier has the right to request a transfer, sir." I had only been in Bravo Company a month, but hated his Napoleonic arrogance and needlessly sacrifices of men.

Our breaths fogged the interior of our rabbit-hole HQ in a snow-covered mountainside. A small oil stove sputtered in the corner.

"You're not going anywhere." He waved a second paper. "You're staying as First Sergeant."

"What...?"

"Your promotion came though."

"I didn't request a damn promotion, sir."

"Well, you've got one, Clooney. You're the most experienced combat noncom I've got since Sgt. Carter bought it." He'd died with Capt. Edwards.

A cold wind knifed through my muddy fatigues and field jacket. I was back from leading a night patrol through another snowstorm. I blew on my numbed hands.

The company clerk eased a cup of steaming coffee in front of Lt. Layton, and looked in my direction. I could have used one.

Layton ignored the gesture.

"Get some chow and get your ass back here

in half an hour, Sergeant..." Layton sucked his pipe, sipped at his coffee and ignored my reluctant salute. "...you've got work to do."

"But, sir—"

"That's all, First Sergeant," he snarled. Layton fought to control his spring-loaded temper. I'd seen him pounce on his men. But he could charm fleas off a dog if he wanted something.

When MacArthur's aide-de-camp inspected our company, Layton brown-nosed, and sucked up like a high-speed vacuum. He charmed the feathers off that bird Colonel, throwing around enough bull about his Senate Armed Services Committee uncle to fertilize Asia.

Within days Lt. Layton became Capt. Layton.

He shined like diamonds in a swamp when a MASH unit arrived Christmas Eve during a snowstorm. We had wounded. Layton bedded the head nurse before dawn in his warm underground quarters, helped by his private hot shower, good chow, and her weakness for nylons and 12-year-old scotch. Don't know where Layton found scotch and nylons in Korea, but he had them. She left before dawn with a hangover, half a case of Johnny Walker Red, and nylon-covered legs.

Layton laughed and bragged about the conquest, and did so in front of his officers and men.

***

I spent a year crawling over the Korean Peninsula, ass-kicking an infantry company. Staying alive wasn't easy.

When Layton made Captain, he became more belligerent, eyeing his next promotion: the silver leaf of a major. He volunteered Bravo for more recons than any other combat company. Our casualties soared.

I hated the cocky SOB, but as First Sergeant I had to back him. I was in the Army, and the bars on Layton's collar outranked my chevrons. It was a pecking order everyone followed, or the military collapsed.

"Captain, these draftees are green." I was protesting another recon. "If I take 'em on patrol, we'll have more cannon fodder. Maybe get me killed, too."

He glared: "HQ doesn't believe our last report."

"We just reconned there," I sighed. "Captain, that's where two rookies bought it; nothing there but landmines, booby traps and bodies. The reds are squirreled-in like Fort Knox."

We lost more good men that night: Cpl. "Dusty" Hammond and Pvt. Vince Drier. Drier had only been in Bravo a week. We were belly-down a mile out when someone sneezed. I don't know who it was. All hell broke loose. I took a round in my right leg. Hammond and Drier vanished under a blanket of mortar shells.

Dusty Hammond's real name was Francis. I didn't know it till I read his 201 File.

The only good that came from that was healing my wounds in an Army hospital outside Tokyo for five weeks. The rooms were warm, the beds soft, and so were the nurses. A slender brunette with inviting green eyes offered to make life easier. I was tempted, but a wife like Catherine doesn't come along every day.

I could have stretched my convalescence with a cushy desk job in Tokyo. My conscience nagged me back to the front, to maybe save some kids from the meat-grinder war.

"First Sergeant!" It was Capt. Rongo Layton. No "Hello," "How are you?" or "Glad to see you." Just his phony alcohol-laced smile.

He unfolded a worn map in the dim light of our underground HQ. A flickering Sterno-burner and gas lantern fought the cold dawn as another storm churned out of Manchuria. I was wearing thick underwear, fatigues, a sweater, a wool scarf, and fur-lined boots, hat, field jacket and gloves. I was still cold. A field radio squawked in the background, controlled by a knob-twisting Signal Corps Private.

Layton smoked his damned MacArthur corncob. I don't know how he could see through those frigging sunglass. MacArthur was a great U.S. General for whipping Japan during WWII, but Layton's adoration was too much.

"HQ wants to know the strength in this sector." Layton's gloved fingers outlined a circle on the map. Beyond flat terrain, a ravine climbed into rugged foothills, ending at enemy lines, marked in red on the map.

"A recon flight could find out," I said.

"Fog's too low," growled Layton. "Planes can't see anything. Too risky."

"Cpl. Sanchez was there two nights ago," I said, studying the map. "Said it was like walking into a Chinese buzz saw; one-way in and one-way out. We'd be sitting ducks."

Our casualties had mounted. We were lucky to hold our lines.

Layton had never been on patrol, or fired a

round in combat. His pistol stayed holstered. He remained in his warm dugout, drinking coffee, smoking, giving orders, and nipping scotch when no one was looking.

"MacArthur thinks the commies are planning a new push." Layton again poked the map. "Needs to know their strength... here."

"We've got nothin' but walking-wounded and wet-nosed draftees, Captain. Gimme a day to—"

"You hard of hearing, Sergeant? Send 'em out. Good OJT. Take Sanchez. He knows the terrain and can help with the new men."

Cpl. Ramon "Rocky" Sanchez, a WWII retread and friend, had seen as much combat as I had. We'd soldiered together in the reserves.

He was short, but muscled, with a grin of perfect white teeth. As a kid his Mexican family had followed California's harvests.

"Never had no cavities," he boasted. "Too poor. Lived on rice, tortillas and beans. You candy-eatin' gringos got the bad teeth. But we got the good choppers and the girls!" Then he laughed as only Rocky could.

We should have all gone AWOL, especially Rocky and Pvt. Rupert L. Maise, because that was the night of the "tripwire" incident.

When I told Sanchez, Layton had ordered him on patrol; he spat toward Layton's dugout. "Lousy bastard! So that's his game."

I didn't understand. I would, later.

Eight of us crawled out of our lines at two in the morning. I took the point. Cpl. Sanchez was the fourth man back. We both carried machine guns, the others, 18- and 19-year-olds, rifles. We squirmed through slush and snow that immediately muddied and soaked us. We crawled toward the enemy lines, carefully skirting a known minefield. Pvt. Maise, a lanky-assed kid from Kansas, hung at my heels. It was his first patrol. It was freezing, but sweat dripped from his chin. The closer we got to the battle lines, the weirder he became. Maise began grinding his teeth, and shaking. He threw up. He began whimpering and babbling, his voice growing louder.

"Shut up!" I growled. I clamped my hand over his mouth.

***

Maise had arrived two weeks earlier, fresh from stateside infantry training. He was scared. All the new men were. He began vomiting, and went on sick call. Claimed stomach cramps and diarrhea.

Layton smiled when seeing replacements sweat.

"Damned malingerers," he'd charged, checking the sick-call roster.

He rode Pvt. Maize and most rookies like a sadistic drill Sergeant. He enjoyed power. Something he proved later with my wife, Catherine.

I was in the mess tent over smokes and coffee with Cpl. Sanchez when Maise returned from sick call for the third time. Capt. Layton chewed his ass. The kid snapped to attention, whiter than bird crap on a statue. I thought he was going to faint.

"I'm... sick, sir," he pleaded. He legs wobbled.

"There will be no shirking in Bravo Company, soldier," snarled Layton. "Not by you, or anyone."

"Not shirking, sir. I'm—"

"You're screwing up my morning report, Pvt. Maise!" Layton shoved a file folder in the kid's clammy face. "Don't like grunts screwing up my paper work!"

"Can't stop throwing up, sir." Maise held up a small bottle of pills. "The medic gave me—"

"You a coward, Private?"

"No, sir." Maise's back was ramrod straight.

Sanchez and I stared from across the mess tent.

"Look at Layton's face," whispered Sanchez.

Layton's temples and eyes bulged, his pupils dilated, his face red. He grinned like an executioner with a dull axe. He ripped into Maise, who remained locked at attention.

"Chewing recruits during basic's one thing," continued Sanchez. "But we're in combat. He's enjoying this."

As senior NCO I walked toward Capt. Layton.

"Sir," I said, "maybe I can handle this—"

I ducked as Layton whirled and swung his fist toward my face. He stopped midway, and slowly unclenched his hand.

"—in your bunker, sir?"

"Stay out of this Sgt. Clooney," he barked. There was no apology. He reeked of alcohol.

***

Capt. Layton had been right about one thing. The fog did roll in like blankets on a bed.

Our patrol was about a hundred yards beyond the minefield when I saw the glint of a tripwire. We were so close to enemy lines I heard guards chattering in Chinese. Using my bayonet I quietly scooped a shallow trench, rolled onto my back, and carefully snaked under the wire. I whispered to Maise to take his time and do the same. Even in the dark I could see his muddy face was paler than when we'd left our lines an hour before.

Then night became day.

Maise had snagged the tripwire with a muddy boot. A million Parachute flares suddenly lighted the sky.

"Get down," I yelled, unnecessary words for the men behind me, now exposed to instant daylight. We didn't move, but remained face down. Not Maise. A strange sound came from his throat as he struggled to his knees under the bright star shells. I tried to grab him, to pull him back into the protective mud and snow. Cpl. Sanchez grabbed his ankle, but Maise twisted free and ran back toward our lines. We tried to cover him with gunfire. Rat-a-tat blasts of enemy machine-gun fire cut him in two.

"Don't anyone move!" My words choked on a mouthful of mud. The earth erupted as more automatic gunfire raked the gully. Screams and moans came from behind me.

Then the flares went out.

"Let's get the hell outta here," I yelled, jumping the tripwire. The others followed, hurrying back to our lines through the fog.

Sanchez didn't make it.

***

"We left four good men out there, Captain," I said an hour later. I'd been crying, but didn't give a damn. I was covered with mud. Shaking and exhausted, I clutched a steaming cup of coffee with both hands. It was the best I'd ever tasted. Everything tastes, smells and feels better after escaping death. Two blankets were draped over my shoulders.

"We don't leave our dead behind, Sgt. Clooney." Capt. Layton had been drinking. A half-empty bottle of scotch was tucked under a nearby blanket. "Doesn't look good at Corps—"

"Screw Corps," I snarled.

"Easy Sergeant!"

"If we'd tried to drag 'em back, we'd all be dead! We couldn't have found all the pieces, Captain. How the hell do you think I feel? Sanchez was my friend."

A slight smile touched Layton's lips. I would soon find out why.

Two of our men had panicked and ran

through the minefield. I could still see their tortured faces. I couldn't remember their names. I was ashamed of that.

They hadn't been in Bravo long enough.

"I yelled at 'em, but they were too scared. The Chinese also dropped a dozen mortars on 'em." I choked, my throat sandpaper dry. A swallow of coffee helped. I'd have gladly accepted his scotch if he'd offered any. He didn't.

The morning sun cut long shadows across the rugged hills. "Only four of us got back, Captain. It was a slaughter! We lost three new grunts and Cpl. Sanchez, the best friend I've got... had," I corrected myself. "We shouldn't have been out there, especially with untested men."

Layton jabbed his corncob in my face: "That's enough, Sgt. Clooney!"

I slapped his pipe aside. I wanted to rip off his sunglasses. Always those damned sunglasses. "I don't give a damn, Captain! You'd have been kinder if you'd just shot 'em!"

"One more word and you're talking court martial!"

"I'd welcome one, sir!"

I glared and placed my hand on a grenade hooked above my breast pocket. Layton backed off.

The company clerk said Layton ranted and raved after I left, kicked over the map table, and stormed out of the bunker.

It was days later when I heard Capt. Layton had borrowed $200 from Cpl. Sanchez.

***

"That your wife, Sergeant?"

Catherine's picture was on my footlocker.

"Yes, sir," I grunted. Dog-tired, I sat on my bunk cleaning my Thompson machine gun. We'd been on another night patrol. Korea's winters were like camping inside a freezer. Fortunately— this time—they'd been no casualties.

Capt. Layton picked up the framed picture of Catherine. She was in a yellow bathing suit sunning on the beach. He gave it a breathy whistle. "Nice. I've always liked blondes. I'll look her up for you when I get home."

He was being reassigned stateside.

I yanked the picture from his hand. "I'd rather you didn't, Captain."

He smiled. I'd soon know way.

I led a three-man patrol the last night of Layton's command. Halfway to our target he launched a series of flares that revealed our location and brought heavy enemy fire. He left before I got back. The company clerk said he'd laughed. Luckily no one was killed. But if I'd found Capt. Layton, I'd have killed him.

Catherine's picture was gone.

Three months later I got a "Dear John" letter. The bastard stole my wife, while I was ducking bullets, nursing recruits, and working on a permanent limp.

Dead buddies, and Capt. Layton stealing Catherine: that's why I hated the man.

Sixty days later I was medevaced home with my third Purple Heart. I'd lost part of my right foot. I received a tearful phone call from Catherine. Layton had dumped her. There had been women, lies, gambling, drugs, and constant drinking.

"He beat me!" she sobbed. "It was awful." She had a black eye and two cracked teeth.

She begged for forgiveness. I don't bend easily. But I did send her some money.

Layton also stole our savings. "Borrowing them," he had told Catherine. There was some justice, because he served a year in Leavenworth for stealing Army funds, and received a Dishonorable Discharge. He then vanished somewhere in the Deep South.

"I don't know where." Catherine wouldn't

stop blubbering.

Two years slid by. She called again. I was retired on full disability, hobbling to physical therapy sessions. The Army said I'd never walk right again.

I was lucky, the doc said. "Got a lifetime pension. That's a million dollar wound you've got, Sergeant."

Catherine wanted back together. There wasn't enough glue in the world to mend that fence. It was too late. The emptiness I'd felt before had grown bigger. Even a friendly dog stays away after its been kicked.

Months later the same VA sawbones dropped another bombshell. I'd been having headaches. Nothing helped. X-rays showed a malignant brain tumor growing faster than our national debt.

"Six months... a year... maybe," they said. "We can give you something for your headaches. It may help."

It didn't.

It's hard to hold back tears when you're dying at forty-two.

I didn't tell Catherine. She had enough troubles.

Twelve months doesn't give you much time

to wrap-up your life.

I now knew where Layton was. A few hundred dollars and a private investigator did the trick.

Layton had stolen my wife and money, killed Cpl. Sanchez, Pvt. Maise and others, and almost got me killed. That's why I was parked in the night shadows outside his home. They say justice is blind. I was about to remove her blindfold, and break her scales. Revenge can be sweet.

I picked up the Magnum, checked its load, neutralized my car's dome-light, and hurriedly limped toward Layton's slowly-closing garage door. I rolled underneath as it thumped into place, missing my gimpy leg.

Rongo Layton left a trail of alcohol fumes and strong pipe smoke as he staggered into his house through his garage. The door slammed behind him, but didn't lock. I'd broken the lock when stealing his Magnum days earlier.

***

"Any last words, my son?" asked the gray-haired priest. A dog-eared Bible occupied his wrinkled hands.

The prisoner shook his head, and rubbed his red eyes.

It was minutes before midnight.

"Have they treated you all right?"

"Yes... yes, sir." Old military habits die hard.

Books and magazines littered the cell's small table. A picture of a beautiful young woman in a yellow bathing suit was taped to the wall.

The convict gestured toward the picture. "Tell... tell Catherine I'm sorry... for everything." His words were barely audible.

A big man in a business suit, flanked by guards, entered the cell.

"It's time!" His voice spilled onto death row.

The shackled prisoner stumbled down the dimly lighted corridor. Guards kept him from falling.

The priest tottered behind, mouthing the 23rd Psalm: "Though I walk through the valley of the shadow of death I will..."

"My life's not suppose to end like this," mumbled the pale convict.

"...fear no evil, for thou art with me..."

He was strapped onto a metal table, needles inserted in his arm. The death chamber's curtains parted, revealing a few chalk-faced guards and reporters. No one else cared.

The chaplain knelt: "It's never too late, my son, to ask for God's forgiveness."

"We fought over the pistol," choked the convict. "He knew my temper... knew I'd lose it. I chased him to his car. He played me. Set me up. Even... even smiled when I shot him."

Tears etched the prisoner's face as he stared at the priest. "May God forgive me, Father, but I believe Sgt. Clooney wanted me to kill him."

Choices

Elizabeth Zelvin

"I shipped out to Nam in '72," I told everyone who asked. "Stayed long enough to sample the dope before the war ended, then we all had to go home." I lied. I got there in '70. Within a month, I'd seen buddies, half my squad, explode in a filthy shower of guts and blood. The rest of us only got back alive by blowing up two villages that supported the Cong. After that, it got worse. By the time I caught the proverbial last helicopter out of Saigon, no picnic either, I was not good company even for myself.

I never did go home, apart from a disastrous visit to my folks when the popping of a champagne cork sent me diving for cover and grabbing for a nonexistent weapon. The girl I'd asked to wait for me recoiled from what she saw lurking behind my eyes.

She knew I was damaged beyond her ability to fix or live with. My heavy drinking had already started, and I wasn't much use to women anyhow. Like other soldiers, I'd taken my turn in line for five minutes with nameless Vietnamese girls. That along with all the rest had made me unfit for tenderness.

I hitched my way to New York, where within a few years of drinking and VA hospital stays, I ended up down on the Bowery. In the Eighties, the Bowery was still Skid Row. I shared a doorway, a cardboard refrigerator box, and a pint of Thunderbird when I had it with a Boston Irish boyo named Danny who taught me how to panhandle. I became a squeegee man, quite the career change. The next decade passed me by in a boozy, soggy blur. It couldn't have rained every day throughout the Eighties, but that's how I remember it.

When I'd had enough of that, I went back to the VA and let them put me through rehab. I had to convince them first that I was motivated. Sure, I was motivated. I had done more than enough research to know that although I'd been able to kill any number of mama-sans when my survival was at stake, I didn't have the guts to jump off the Brooklyn Bridge. Or maybe that's not a contradiction. For some crazy reason, I never stopped wanting to survive. At the VA, I straightened up enough to hold a real job, if you can call bartending that. It worked for me. I could maintain a buzz and still come across as respectable. I made enough to pay the rent on a crummy walk-up apartment on the edge of Chinatown. I could fool the fools who spent their evenings at my bar that I was civilized. Most days I still woke up wondering why I bothered.

Every once in a while, one of the regulars would take the AA route. They'd drop by all shiny with sobriety and try to talk me into doing the same.

"I swear to you, Larry," they'd say, "the program works. My worst day sober is better than my best day drinking. You should try it."

"Thanks, man," I'd say. "Congratulations and all that, but it's not for me." I didn't try to explain the catch to them. See, they had no idea what a real worst day could be. It was a nice bar, on the Upper East Side. They were all yuppies: lawyers, bank officers, computer programmers. Their idea of a bad day was rushing into court without their tie. A worse day would be getting chewed out for interrupting the judge. They might pay $12.50 to see a horror movie, and I knew they did—everyone's a critic in a bar—but if they could attend a screening of my memories, they'd want their money back.

So the years rolled by. My back got stiffer, my hands slower, my nightmares less frequent as time passed. I got used to smoking out on the sidewalk instead of inside the bar. I got used to the parade of yuppies looking younger every year. I even got used to the regulars calling me Pops instead of Larry. But nothing of any significance ever changed until I met Nellie.

It wasn't what you think. Nellie was young enough to be my daughter and then some. I carded her the first time she walked into the bar. She argued when I asked for her ID and got indignant when I raised an eyebrow at her stated age of 23. Nellie had an innocence to match her old-fashioned name in spite of her tattoos and the expanse of bare midriff between her cropped tops and low-cut jeans. She wasn't a real drinker. She could nurse a Miller Lite for an hour, forgetting it altogether while she engaged in conversation with whoever happened to be propping up the bar on a given night. She was a good listener. When one of the regulars started a story I'd heard too many times, I'd point to where she perched with her elbows on the bar.

"I'm referring you a client," I'd call out.

"Thanks, Larry," she'd say. "The shrink is

in." She never called me Pops.

Then one night, Nellie came in late with a package under her arm. It was raining hard outside. I'd heard the crack of thunder when it started, and people had been stomping in shaking off water like dogs for the past hour. One way heavy drinkers are like soldiers: they don't go in for umbrellas. Nellie had a pink one, but it had obviously been killed in action. She tossed it into the big trash can by the entrance and came toward me, hugging whatever it was to her chest. It was about the size of a shoebox, but flatter, with rounded corners. It was wrapped in black plastic, probably a giant garbage bag, and secured with rubber bands. Her brown hair hung down over her face and shoulders in dripping rat tails. She wasn't wearing a jacket, and her clothes were drenched. She cocked her head at me and hopped onto a stool at the empty end of the bar, still hugging the package.

I put down the glass I'd been polishing and moved toward her.

"Nellie. Nice night for ducks." I'd been saying it all evening. "What'll it be?" My usual patter. It meant nothing. Like soothing a dog: Good boy, come on now. She always had a Miller Lite, anyhow.

"Larry. I need your help." Her voice came out strained and husky. Her teeth chattered as she held out the package, glistening with wet. "Can you hold onto this for me?" The package shook a little in her hands.

"Sure, darlin'." I poured her a beer even though she frowned and jerked her chin sideways as I pushed it toward her. "What is it?"

"I can't tell you. I just need you to hang onto it for a while. I—I'm not sure how long. Put it somewhere safe for me. Please!"

"Hey, hey there, darlin'. Don't get your panties in a twist. Good girl. Come on now, Larry's got your back, no sweat. What's going on?" I reached across the bar and took her chin gently between my fingers so I could look her in the eyes.

"I can't tell anyone. I don't even know—" He eyes were huge dark pools. "Oh, God, I can't do this. Larry, can I trust you?"

I could smell the fear coming off her. If the bar hadn't been between us, I'd have given her a hug, if I'd been the hugging kind of guy. I straightened up and snapped her a salute, probably standing taller than I had in years. I hoped to make her smile, but instead her eyes welled up and overflowed with tears.

62

"Hey, hey, Nellie, it's okay, it's gonna be all right, darlin'." Leaning over the bar, I laid my big hands on her shivering shoulders as gently as I could. I even stroked her back a little, hoping she wouldn't mind or misunderstand. More important, my back was broad enough to hide her from the room. "Sure you can trust me. Old soldiers never die, we just get very, very quiet. Tell me what's wrong, and we'll figure out together what to do."

"I didn't know you were a soldier." She wiped the palm of her hand across her face, leaving a trail of snot along her upper lip. On her it looked endearing, like a little kid's milk mustache.

"Yeah, I don't exactly advertise." As her face changed, I added, "Hey, it's okay! I only meant that if you need protecting, I'm your man." I wanted to reassure myself as well as her. Who knew if I was still operational? I hadn't checked my skills out in a long time. "Why don't you go ahead and tell me all about it? Here, give me that." I plucked the package from her sheltering arms and tucked it down beneath the bar. "See? Load lightened already. Now what the hell's happened that's got you running so scared?"

One damp hand crept out and curled around my neck to draw me closer. It was the first time she had touched me. For a moment, I flashed on carrying my sister's little girl to bed, a good moment in that painful visit home after I came back from Nam. Not my usual flashback by a long shot. I leaned in until our foreheads were no more than an inch apart. I could feel her warm breath tickling my chin.

"My sister's dead," she whispered. Not at all what I expected, whatever that might have been. "I never told you about my sister. I don't talk about her much. We used to be very close. That's why—well, when we hung out, that's when I kinda got used to bars. Stephanie's an alcoholic."

I didn't flinch, but it took an effort. A combat soldier's got to be a rock. I was out of practice.

"She's an addict too, she's been—she got hooked on heroin for a while, then she got into coke. Lately it's just been crack, because it's cheaper. She can't—she couldn't hold a job any more."

"And you've been taking care of her?" I prompted.

"Well, yes and no. I've been trying not to

enable. See, I've been going to Al-Anon."

"I know about Al-Anon," I said. It's AA for folks who know someone who drinks too much. They learn it's not their fault. I'd never understood the point of it, to tell the truth.

"But she's my sister. I don't give her money any more, because I know where it goes. But I can't—couldn't—let her sleep on the street, could I? So I—I let her stay on my couch."

"Uh huh, of course you would. Go on. What happened?"

"She stayed with me last weekend, but then she took off. I didn't see her for three days. That was the way it was, she'd pop in and out, I'd never know if she was still alive." Her breath caught on a sob. She took a deep breath to quiet it.

"Don't worry," I said, "no one's looking or listening."

"When I got home from work tonight, she was there. She was all lit up—I mean, I knew she must be on something, but she was also excited. Elated. She told me I could stop worrying about her, because she'd done something really smart for a change, and now she'd be able to take care of herself. She wouldn't tell me what it was, but when I asked if she'd signed up for rehab, she laughed at me really hard. What would the opposite of rehab be?"

"Hmm." I didn't have to think about it long. "A really big score."

"That's what I was afraid of."

The next question was obvious: What was in that package? But she hadn't yet told me how her sister turned up dead. I nodded at her to go on.

"She wanted to take off, but I talked her into letting me make her dinner. She would never eat unless someone prodded her. She was like that from the time she was a little girl. It wasn't just the drugs. But she was thin as a stick, and I worried about her."

"You're a nice girl, Nellie."

"Yeah, well, I screwed up. If I hadn't made her stay for dinner—if I hadn't been out of garlic—if I hadn't run out to the store to get some—she wouldn't have been dead when I got back!" Sobs threatened to overwhelm her. She forced them back.

"I bet in Al-Anon they'd say it wasn't your fault."

I glanced over my shoulder, wondering why nobody had been hollering at me for a drink. I saw that the kid who sometimes helped out at the bar had come in and was taking care of the customers. Good. He was the landlord's nephew, about Nellie's age, and his ambition seemed to be to twirl two beer bottles like a drum majorette, the way Tom Cruise did in that stupid movie. I'd only seen it on the TV in the bar. Maybe it was better with the sound on, but I doubted it.

"Yeah, you're right, they would. But I still blame myself."

"Dead how?" I kept my voice low, though the noise in the room was loud enough to cover our voices. The rain had driven a lot of folks besides the regulars in for a drink.

"Did she OD? Kill herself?"

"No! If it had been either of those, I'd have called 911, and I wouldn't have left the apartment. Someone killed her!"

A nice girl like Nellie would have called 911 to report a murder under normal circumstances. The circumstances must not have been normal.

"How? Was she stabbed? Shot? Beaten up?"

"I think she was shot." Her lip quivered. "I know she was shot. There was a hole behind her ear and a funny smell."

"Why did you leave?" I had to ask.

"It was my father's gun," she said in a small voice. "He brought it back from Vietnam."

"Are you saying it was lying there?"

"No. It was missing. I never touched it, but Stephanie knew where I kept it, in a hat box on top of the closet. I think she took it out and loaded it to protect herself. So nothing would happen. Oh, God, don't let me cry, I'll never get through this if I break down."

"We'll get through it together," I said. It seemed the right time to ask my question. "What's in the package?" It was a multiple choice question, anyhow. "Drugs or money?"

"Money," she said. "A lot of money. I only opened it enough to get a peek, but it was all hundreds, and look at the size of it."

"You could still have called the cops," I said. I'd never called a cop in my life, not even to ask directions. But Nellie wasn't the type to go on the lam with stolen money. "Why didn't you?"

"I was afraid that whoever killed her would come back before the cops arrived. They found the gun, but they tore the place apart looking for the money, and they didn't find it. I think she was alive while they were looking. She was—" she closed her eyes as if to pray for strength to finish the sentence—"tied. And—and—"

68

She couldn't go on, and I didn't make her. I could fill in the blank myself: tortured.

"You couldn't have helped," I said gently. "Try not to think about it."

I should know, having spent decades destroying my body and my character rather than think about my own experiences of the same kind. Except I hadn't always been on the receiving end. When I said I couldn't get sober, I wasn't blowing off a golden opportunity. I was putting up a shield between myself and hell. I had no choice.

"Can you stand one more question?" I asked Nellie.

"Sure, why not." She rocked back on the bar stool, hugging her arms. Her pale face, streaked with tears and snot and mascara smudges, made her look like a raccoon, but it wasn't remotely funny.

I had to think about how to say it without getting graphic.

"How come they didn't get the hiding place out of Stephanie?"

She went even paler as she unfolded her arms and put her hands flat out on the bar, as if she didn't think she deserved a hug even from herself.

"Stephanie was a really, really good liar. When she swore to you black was white, you could see that she believed herself while she was saying it. It was in a much better hiding place than the gun. It's my secret cache for, you know, a little good jewelry that belonged to my mother, whatever. I didn't think she even knew about it, but she must have snooped and seen me some other time."

"She hid the money there, so she could have told them where it was. I'm sorry, Nellie, but they could have made her tell them."

"But she didn't," Nellie said. "I think she told them she'd given it to me to hide. Stephanie was like that. She loved me, but she had no moral fiber. No center. I think she told them I was the only one who knew."

If she couldn't point them to the money, Stephanie was valueless to them. So they shot her. And now they'd be coming after Nellie.

"I wonder why they didn't hide out and wait for you to come back."

"I thought about that." She lifted her chin. "I bet Stephanie told them I was out of town or something. She wasn't evil, you know, just weak. Fatally weak. And she was high at the time. That's not weakness. It's a disease, you know."

"Yeah, yeah. If they didn't believe her, they'll come back. You can't go home."

"I know. They might not even have gone far, just beyond where anyone who might have heard the shot would tell the cops to look. That's why I came to you."

"Don't you have any friends?" I asked.

"I didn't want to put them in danger," she said. "I mean, I don't mean I don't care about you, I do, it's just that—" She spluttered to a halt.

I grinned.

"I know. You figured I could take care of myself. Don't worry, darlin', you were right about that."

At that moment, I could kind of understand what she'd said about Stephanie. I had to say it, so when I said it, I'd better believe it. And when she looked at me with perfect trust in her eyes, it wasn't just a fancy kind of lie.

"Tell me what to do, Larry. What now?"

"We have choices," I said, putting all the firmness I could muster in my voice. I could take care of myself. And dammit, I'd take care of Nellie too or die trying.

"We?" she said, the first little smile of the evening quirking up her lips.

"Yep."

"We have choices," she repeated. "Funny, that's what they say in Al-Anon. Okay, Larry, what are our choices?"

"If those goons had followed you here, they'd have busted in and shot up the place by now. That means we can assume they don't know where you are. So you're safe as long as you're here."

"I felt safe the moment I walked in and saw you," Nellie said. "It just took me a little while to get over being scared."

"We can call the cops now," I said. "Tell them your story, and wait right here till they arrive."

"The whole story?"

"Sure," I said. "Or you could leave the gun out of it. It being your father's and all. You have choices."

"Okay," she said. "What else?"

"Look." I beckoned her closer, so she could see down into the well beneath the bar. I kept a couple of baseball bats there, along with an iron crowbar and a Colt .45, an M1911 that I'd kept when I came back from Nam. I'd somehow managed to hold onto it through all my travels. "We can go back to your apartment, wait for the bad guys to come back, and give 'em hell."

72

"Me too?"

"Hmm." I hadn't thought that one through. "I don't want you getting hurt. I could choose to leave you here, or you could wait in a safe hiding place and give me the nod when they show up."

"And I could choose to stay with you," she said. "My dad taught us both how to shoot."

Let her take the gun? I'd been trained in unarmed combat and used it plenty, but it had been a long time. Having to look out for her at the same time might slow me down.

"What if you missed?"

"I wouldn't miss." Her jaw clenched. She looked like a kitten trying to be tough, but somehow I believed her. "Those goons killed my sister."

"I'd still have a choice," I admitted, "between a crowbar and a baseball bat." I wasn't ready to tell her how good I'd once been at killing with my bare hands.

"I used to be pretty damn good at stickball."

This time her grin lit up the room. Or maybe it was my imagination. I couldn't help smiling in return.

"Enough choices for you, ma'am?" I asked.

"You forgot one."

"What's that?"

"We can take that bundle of you-know-what, grab a cab out to the airport, and catch the next flight to Rio. Or Paris, if you'd rather. Have you ever been to Paris?"

I shook my head. I'd had all the foreign travel I needed, thank you, before 1973. I had kept my passport current, though. I guess I'd wanted to believe I had choices all along. It was a catch she probably hadn't thought of.

"Not so fast," I said. "I bet you don't even have a passport."

"You'd be wrong," she crowed. "It was in the cache, and I snatched it up and took it along, I don't know why. Instinct."

"Rio, huh." I told myself I was only playing along. "I don't know about South America. The bad guys might have buddies there."

"The South Pacific, then," she said. "I kind of like the sound of Bora Bora."

I sure had been wrong about her not going on the lam. I'd have trouble keeping up with her.

"But it's only fair to tell you I won't sleep with you—" She held up one hand to stop me, though I wasn't going to interrupt, my jaw hadn't finished dropping yet. "—until you've been to three AA meetings and commit to a goal of 90 days sober. One day at a time, of course. No one expects you to do more than that."

I guess she didn't see me as a father. I'd been wrong about that too. I opened my mouth to tell her why I could never get sober, and found myself saying instead, "They have AA in Bora Bora?"

"Well, somewhere in Tahiti, anyway. Why not? And if they don't, we'll go somewhere else. We have choices."

While I hesitated, she hopped down from the bar stool and started toward the door, turning back when she realized I still stood, flummoxed, behind the bar.

"What are you waiting for?" Her feet, her eyes, her hair, which had dried in little ringlets, everything about her seemed to be dancing. "Grab your passport and the you-know-what, leave the gun—you'll never get it through security—and let's go! We've got a plane to catch!"

I guess I'd been wrong about a lot of things.

The Gift of Life

Lina Zeldovich

Johnnie Summers sat down on the concave
yellow seat of the N train heading toward
Manhattan from Astoria, dubbed the United
Nations of New York City. Hispanics, Greeks,
Arabs, Eastern Europeans and Midwesterners
favored this Queens neighborhood for its
proximity to Midtown, cheap rents, good food
and nightlife. Johnnie grew up in rural
Oklahoma and always wanted to live in a big
city, so once he was discharged from the army he
settled in the biggest city he could.

Before the train's door closed, a young girl
sat down next to him, her head wrapped in a
blue headscarf, a few safety pins holding it in
place, not a hair peeking from underneath.
Definitely of Islamic faith, she was dressed in
free flowing clothes designed to conceal her body
rather than flaunt it. Even her delicate pink
fingers seemed to hide inside her wide sleeves.
After two years of dealing with Pashtun's

Namus, a woman's honor code and ethics, Johnnie knew better than to stare at a Muslim female. He only threw one quick glance at her–and started.

The girl looked just like Jamila. She had the same huge green eyes–color of liquid emeralds, framed by thick long lashes. Two perfectly formed arches of her eyebrows curved over her eyes and her red lips bloomed on her golden skin like spring poppies in the Afghan steppes.

The girl noticed his stare and inched away.

"I'm sorry," Johnnie mumbled hoarsely. "I didn't mean to... It's just that you look like... someone I used to know."

"It's OK, some people look alike," the girl answered in perfect American English. "Does she live around here?"

"Uh, no." Johnnie cleared his throat. "That was in Afghanistan. Is that where you are from?"

"No," the girl shook her head with a subdued smile. Johnnie realized she was as flattered by his attention as she was embarrassed. "My family's from Pakistan."

"You live here now?"

She nodded. "My father owns the grocery shop on the corner of Thirty First Avenue and

Steinway. And I go to LaGuardia."

Johnnie was new to New York, but he remembered seeing posters for La Guardia Community College in Queens.

"That's good," he said and nodded, not knowing what to say next. He was still in awe of her striking semblance to Jamila and her rare beauty. "I'm Johnnie."

She wouldn't shake his hand, but she gave him a big joyful smile. "I'm Fatima."

***

The Hanshin castle sat in the middle of Helmand province–the southwest part of Afghanistan. Looking more like a dilapidated caravanserai than a fortress, the castle towered on a hill overlooking a sprawl of desiccated land that separated a small Pashtun village from the Helmand valley. Behind the village was a mine field leftover from the Soviet occupation, and the children knew to keep away from its broken barbed wire as soon as they learned to walk on their skinny legs.

In spring the Helmand River flooded, turning the dreary sand into a pink-red carpet of blooming poppies. The coalition forces seized the area from the Taliban and turned the castle into a Forward Operating Base to keep

Helmand—Afghanistan's drug capital which produced most of the world's opium—under control.

The poppies were in bloom, but it wasn't the picturesque landscape that caught Johnnie's eye from the castle wall. He had spotted a civilian car on the dirt road down below, enveloped in a cloud of dust that even spring rains couldn't extinguish. Cars were scarce. Donkeys were cheap.

"Yo, Scraggy," he called out to the Pashtun village boy who had gotten himself adopted by the base, helping with chores in exchange for food and small change. His father had been killed by the Taliban so he was now supporting his family. "Is that old Soviet Volga coming to your village?"

"Uncle Hassan's niece Jamila," Scraggy said. "Most beautiful girl in all Kabul."

Scott Roberts, Johnnie's bunk mate, spat out his chewed up cigarette butt and joined the conversation.

"What's the most beautiful girl in all Kabul doing in this frigging place? At least there she could've made herself a few bucks." He grinned. "No high-paying clientele here."

"Parents die in a blast," Scraggy said. His

English wasn't yet good enough to fully understand Scott's insulting remark so his Pashtun pride was not offended. "Come live with uncle."

Driving on patrol two weeks later, Johnnie and Scott passed through the village, followed by a tail of unwashed boys in soiled *payraans*–long overshirts, and girls in *chaadars*–colorful headscarves. Scott steered while Johnnie threw candy to the kids, who shouted *"Tashakor"*– thank you. Johnnie noticed a female figure wrapped in an unusually richly decorated chaadar, huddling under a crooked tree.

"Candy!" he shouted to her and summoned his rudimentary knowledge of the local dialect. *"Gaaz!"*

The girl approached them hesitantly, eyes cast down and hiding behind her chaadar sewn with colorful rhinestones. Her fingers slipped from her long sleeve and grasped the Kit Kat. When she finally looked up, mouthing a quiet "Thank you, sir," her English was nearly perfect as if she had spoken it her entire life. But it wasn't her English that took Johnnie's breath away.

It was her eyes. Her eyes were huge, taking almost her entire face and shining through the opening of her chaadar so brilliantly green they were brighter than poppies after the spring showers, brighter than emeralds, brighter than anything Johnnie had ever seen.

"Whoa," Scot breathed out next to him, his own eyes wide-open in awe. "Christ, I've never seen eyes so gorgeous before. Take that stupid thing off, would you?"

But Jamila, scared by their reaction, which she understood all too well, was already running back to her uncle's house. Scott threw the truck in gear to follow her, but Johnnie grabbed the wheel.

"Don't even think about it," he snapped. "Go back to the base."

***

Their schedules seemingly in sync, Johnnie and Fatima met on the platform and rode together talking non-stop every morning. They talked about Pakistan versus America, Islam versus Christianity, Urdu versus English, and lamb kebobs versus steaks. It was a strange friendship which they both enjoyed.

Her life views shaped by both her family beliefs and America society, Fatima was a peculiar mix of East and West. She deemed her headscarf a fashion statement, insisted that

Islam was a peaceful religion turned into a weapon by fanatical clergymen and believed in both the woman's right to work and arranged marriages. She was well-read, inquisitive and far more interesting than hip American chicks Johnnie picked up in bars and nightclubs. They wanted a guy with deep pockets and disappeared after a few dates. Finding the right girl wasn't easy.

"In my culture, you'd go to your parents and tell them you are ready," Fatima told him one morning. "They'd find you the right girl."

Johnnie imagined his mother looking for a bride in his Oklahoma home town and felt the hairs on his back bristle. "What if I don't like their choice? How would they know what I want in a girl?"

"They'd listen to your opinion," Fatima assured him. "But they would know better than you. They're older. They understand what works and what doesn't."

Johnnie pictured himself talking to his imaginary Muslim parents. Since he wouldn't have had any pre-marital sexual experience, they'd be indeed superior to him in their knowledge. The vision wasn't particularly pleasant.

"What if your parents tell you they have a husband for you tomorrow?" Johnnie asked.

Fatima giggled. "I don't want kids yet. Maybe in five years, or at least when I finish school. My parents know I'm not ready–I'm still underage."

"How old are you?" Johnnie asked, surprised. He had always thought of Fatima being in her early twenties. She was so bright, mature and adult-like.

"Fifteen," she answered, getting up as the train approached the Queens Plaza station where she had to change for another train.

"What?" Johnnie asked in awe. "You said you go to LaGuardia College."

"Oh, no!" Fatima laughed like a chorus of silvery bells. "I go to LaGuardia High School. La Guardia High School of Art."

She ran across the platform to catch her train.

***

In the beginning of July Scraggy brought news of the village young men going *khastegari* to Uncle Hassan–asking for Jamila's hand in marriage.

"Isn't she still a kid?" Johnnie asked. "She barely looked sixteen to me."

Scraggy shook his head. "She fourteen. My sister marry at twelve. Her husband thirty four."

Johnnie shook his head. "Christ. He'd be in jail in my country."

Scraggy didn't know the word jail so he smiled.

"Jamila speaks English, huh?" Scott asked, leaning on the white castle wall, built from horse hair, straw and mud.

Scraggy nodded. "She go to school in Kabul. Her father was University professor, mother teacher. She want be teacher too."

Scott cursed and lit a cigarette. "One of these dirty monkeys will get to screw that little body while looking into those gorgeous eyes. I could frigging kill to see that face."

"Drop it," Johnnie snapped. "You know you're asking for trouble."

"Sure," Scott said unpleasantly. "So who's gonna be the lucky man?"

Scraggy said that Uncle Hassan had promised his niece to the shoemaker's son, but then the old Khaleed Hajib interfered. It was against the tradition to argue over an agreed marriage, but the man had pull.

Still childless at fifty-five, Khaleed had buried three wives. Rumor had it, he had beaten

84

them to death once they failed to produce kids. Worse, he was a Taliban supporter and until the coalition took over he had proudly displayed a *"Zenda baad Taliban"* banner in his window–"Long live the Taliban."

"You gotta be kidding me," Scott muttered, unbelieving. "Hassan may as well kill Jamila than give her to that pig!"

"People afraid Khaleed Hajib," Scraggy explained. "Taliban may come back."

"Taliban ain't coming back," Scott shouted. "We threw their asses outta here for good. Tell Uncle Hassan he has nothing to worry about. If he has to marry off his niece, let him at least find a guy who doesn't beat his wives into the ground."

Johnnie didn't think Scraggy understood much of Scott's fervent speech.

"Jamila beautiful," the boy said, his crooked teeth showing in a smile he meant to be soothing. "Women give gift of life. She give Khaleed a son–he no beat but love her."

***

One morning Fatima and Johnnie had a heated discussion over the fact that the Quran allowed a man to have four wives.

"Polygamy is not a uniquely Islamic

concept," Fatima argued with Johnnie, her ardent green eyes glowing with righteous anger. "Have you read your Christian Bible? How many wives did the kings Solomon and David have?"

"It's different," Johnnie tried to explain his point of view. "Those are old stories. No one takes them seriously. No one marries multiple women in Western society."

"It's just as uncommon in Pakistan," Fatima told him. "But many Americans seem to think Muslim women are kept prisoners in their harems. Look, I walk around by myself and I talk to whoever I want. You guys think you know everything about us, but you really don't."

Johnnie opened his mouth to rebut her statement, but the train doors opened and the crowd poured in from the platform, bringing in a tall stocky man in Middle-Eastern clothes, in need of a shave and haircut. He saw Fatima and Johnnie talking and his eyes ignited in an instant, burning with a gamut of emotions—everything from terror to disgust to fury.

Sputtering curses Johnnie couldn't understand, the man yanked Fatima from her seat so fast she was nearly suspended in the air for a few moments. She talked back in Urdu as she tried to free her arm, and although Johnnie didn't know what she said, he knew what the argument was about. Fatima was caught talking to a male who wasn't family, but rather a loose American with no concept of female honor and undoubtedly bad intentions.

Johnnie threw himself at the man, grabbing him by the shirt.

"Let her go, asshole, or I'll break your neck!"

The man stared at Johnnie, willing to be killed rather than let go of Fatima's hand. Johnnie's hand formed a fist, and he nearly punched the guy out, but Fatima hung on his arm, her voice pleading guiltily.

"Please don't! He's my uncle."

***

Later in July, the castle personnel embarked on a restoration effort. Huge holes in the walls left from the air strikes were to be mended. Broken staircases were to be fixed. A recreational room was being built where soldiers would watch satellite TV and play electronic games.

Squatting next to the ivory wall, Johnnie was diligently filling a hole with cement when he realized Scott was no longer jabbering next to him. Johnnie looked around, expecting to find

Scott napping underneath the sad-looking trees that survived enemy fire, but he was nowhere in sight. Instead, Johnnie saw a small female figure wrapped in the familiar lavishly decorated chaadar, walking through the wilted poppies down below with a basket of food from the valley market. A second later he saw Scott running along the barbed wire fence after her.

"Shit," Johnnie hollered as he jumped over the unfinished wall. "What the hell are you're doing?"

Johnnie thought he ran faster than he did under enemy fire, yet he wasn't fast enough. When he reached the poppy field, the scene was already a disaster, at least by the Pashtun Namus code. Caught on the barbed wire, Jamila's chaadar whipped in the wind, her overturned basket thrown in the sand. Her little round face, uncovered and exposed, looked like an apple in Scott's huge hands He brushed her raven hair off her forehead, spilling it over her shoulders like a black waterfall as he bent down to kiss her.

Johnnie smashed into Scott like a missile hitting its target, knocking him onto the hot sand and landing on top. Scott pushed him off, but Johnnie tripped him before he got onto his feet. For the next few minutes they hit, punched and pummeled each other, until Johnnie hit Scott hard enough to send him reeling backwards. Scott crashed into the barbed fence. The wire, already broken in several places, gave way, taking Scott with it onto the other side of the fence, into the mine field.

He was still falling, his elbow an inch away from the ground, when Johnnie grabbed his other hand, leaving him suspended in air.

Ten minutes later they were still sitting next to each other on the hot sand amongst the wilted leaves and dry poppy heads, scared of what could've happened. Jamila had long run away, but a small rhinestone from her chaadar twinkled in the sand and a scrap of silk caught in the fence whipped in the wind like a lost memory.

***

Fatima no longer took the train in the morning. No matter how long Johnnie waited for her on the platform she never showed up. Johnnie found her father's store on the corner of Thirty First Avenue and Steinway, and began patronizing it for newspapers and cigarettes, hoping to run into Fatima one day. Two weeks later he succeeded. She was behind the counter and alone.

Alarm flashed across Fatima's face when she saw Johnnie.

"You have to leave!" she spat out at him, her frightened version of a hello. Her usual mirth was gone. She looked like a scared bird. "I'll be in so much trouble if my father sees you."

"Your father has seen me," Johnnie said dismissively. "I come every day. I'm a customer. There's nothing wrong with you talking to a customer."

"Yes, but..."

"How come I never see you on the train anymore?"

Fatima avoided his eyes. "They're just afraid that... I may do something stupid. Young people do sometimes."

"But you weren't doing anything stupid," Johnnie protested. "All we did was talk. I am sorry you got in trouble because of me, but your parents have no right to lock you up. You always said they were modern and understanding."

"They are, but my uncle isn't," Fatima uttered. She looked away, biting her lips. "He's very religious and takes Namus very seriously."

"Are they letting you go to school?" Johnnie demanded. "Because if they aren't the school will find out. They'll come to your house."

Fatima stared into the floor. "My uncle told the school we moved to another city."

It finally hit Johnnie. "They're marrying you off, aren't they?"

Fatima gave off a tremor and he knew he was right.

"It's illegal," he yelled. "Your husband will go to jail and so will your parents for forcing you into it. Don't tell me you agreed!"

Fatima's huge green eyes were larger than ever, full of pain and sorrow and tears.

"I didn't want to," she started. Her voice trailed off. "I tried to fight but.... He's my cousin, I'd marry him in a few years anyway."

"There's a difference!" Johnnie yelled, outraged. "In a few years you will be of legal age. Right now you're still a kid. Don't let them do it to you!"

"They won't listen," Fatima moaned. "They're scared. My uncle told them I'll turn out just like the loose Western girls. I don't know what to do!"

"Maybe I can help!" Impulsively, Johnnie grabbed Fatima's hand and she recoiled. Her face turned red and a tear slid down her cheek, clear like a drop of dew on a blooming poppy.

"Please go," she whispered. "This is not a

battle a soldier can win."

***

The horse, decorated with colorful fabrics, ribbons and bows, carried Jamila to her husband's home. A flock of kids chased the wedding procession, hooting and singing. The village musicians blew the thin *shahnai* flutes and beat the *dohol* drums. Before Scraggy left the base to join the celebration, he had briefed the soldiers on a traditional Afghan wedding. He had said Jamila had signed the *Nikaah*–the marriage contract. The village women painted her hands with henna. Her hair was parted with silver dust and arranged in beautiful braids, held together by tree sap. She wore beautiful jewelry, which Khaleed bought her as a wedding present. Now it was her turn to give him a great gift. A gift of life–a son.

Scott and Johnnie watched the festivities from behind the Hanshin walls.

"I can't believe this shit," Scott muttered grimly. "A coupla good rounds–that's what the asshole deserves. Instead he gets that beauty. These people are so backwards."

"It's their customs," Johnnie uttered morosely. "It's their country. We're not to interfere."

"We're liberating them, for chrissake!" Scott glared at the celebrating crowd. "She's fourteen and she's marrying a fifty-year old murderer of three wives. She'll be dead by Ramadan!"

"You're a soldier, not a marriage counselor," Johnnie barked, the disturbing image gnawing at his brain. He was mad at Scott and sick of his own helplessness. "There're battles you can't win."

Down below the men started dancing *Attan*—the traditional communal dance performed in a circle. Scott squinted at the bouncing crowd trying to pinpoint Jamila's husband.

"Nothing that a good sniper rifle can't fix," he muttered. "And I've got one, too. How about giving Jamila a gift of life?"

Johnnie opened his mouth to answer, but didn't say anything. He finished his cigarette and went back to the barracks where he plopped onto his bunk and fell asleep.

It was a few hours later that a mine went off, rocking the castle like an earthquake and forcing the personnel to instantly take cover. Since no more blasts followed, an all-clear sounded shortly. It was not the enemy who set the mine off. When the first rays of sun licked the earth, a group of villagers crowded at the barbed wire fence, staring at the new crater while the wind tossed the green scraps of an Afghan wedding gown over the burnt land.

***

Parked a block away from Fatima's home, Johnnie watched the groom and his family arrive and enter the house, welcomed by their prospective in-laws. Following a short welcoming reception, Fatima would sign her marriage Nikaah, after which she and her husband would see each other's faces in the mirror slipped underneath her veils. A *mullah* would recite a prayer from the Quran and there would be no way back.

Johnnie stepped out of the car and walked to Fatima's house. He had shunned this battle once before, but he wouldn't this time. Here, on the red brick steps, he mentally switched from civilian mode back into a soldier. His face changed. His senses sharpened. Every nerve and muscle in his body went on high alert. He cleared his head from any concerns about customs and traditions as if he operated under a military order. He took his gun off safety and kicked in the door.

The house was a maze of small rooms crammed with furniture. As Johnnie expected, the first room he found was full of men. Loud and cheerful, the men instantly went silent in horror. The groom trembled in his richly decorated wedding costume and grabbed his dad's hand. Fatima's father wheezed. Her uncle glared at Johnnie with almost palpable hatred.

"Nobody move," Johnnie declared and he backed into the next room, his gun pointed at the horrified groom. Somewhere in this house there was a room full of women and Johnnie was determined to find it.

The chatter and giggles died as he broke into the small space smelling of turmeric, sandalwood and aromatic oils. Dressed up in lavishly decorated and embroidered gowns, the women looked like dolls with their eyes rounded in terror. Before anyone drew a breath, Johnnie scanned the room, saw a pair of sad green eyes behind a transparent veil, lifted Fatima off her seat and carried her out on his arm like a jinn from a Middle-Eastern tale.

He knew he'd be attacked in the all-male room on his way out, but his combat skills never dulled. In a series of quick moves, he shoved his elbow into Fatima's father's solar plexus, careful not to injure but only immobilize the man, sent another relative reeling into a wall and delivered a blow across her uncle's throat finishing him off with the butt of his gun.

"You touch her—you're dead," Johnnie growled when the furious groom blocked his way, the gun's black nozzle an inch away from the guy's head, and backed out onto the street.

He drove through two red lights at double the speed limit, until he was satisfied no cars were following them. Fatima sat next to him, still in shock.

"Where are you taking me?" she asked when she regained her speech. Dressed in the shimmering red dress sown with sequins and diamantes, with heavy jewels and hands painted with henna, she looked like an ancient princess who had accidentally stepped off an old painting.

"Child services," Johnnie said. "They'll talk to your family so you don't have to. You don't belong to their tribal lifestyle. You are your own person."

"My mother will be happy," Fatima whispered. Her multi-layered gold earrings gave off a faint jingle. "She didn't want to give me away. Maybe my father will understand too."

Johnnie heard a faint cadence of relief in

her voice and knew he had won at least one battle. Maybe the best one ever.

"Why did you do this?" Fatima asked.

Johnnie thought of the red poppies, barbed wire fences and the flock of unwashed kids watching the wind blow around pieces of green silk. He wasn't good with words so his answer was simple.

"To give you the gift of life."

Justice at Sea

Charles Schaeffer

Beginning in the Solomon Islands, the lengthy sea journey—one day of tedium following hard on the heels of another—ended at last. Ahead loomed their frightful destination: Corregidor, a stark monolith, thrusting from the ocean like a massive breaching whale.

Topside on the cruiser USS Flagstaff, Johnny Shepherd watched the convoy's warships, one by one, zero in on the Japanese-held redoubt. Puffs of white smoke followed by thunder of exploding shells pocked the island's rugged sides. One of the Flagstaff's six-inch guns angled up and fired a shell whistling toward its target. Shepherd's ears rang as he watched a machine-gun pattern of splashes respond, racing toward the ship. Gunbursts winked in the distance. The Japanese were shooting at the Flagstaff—at him—he ducked behind a lifeboat, scared, but hypnotized by the exploding landscape.

Overhead, the air bloomed with mushroom parachutes gliding toward the hostile surface of Corregidor. One by one, Army paratroopers drifted down. Gunfire flashed back, and, now and then, Shepherd winced as a taut airborne body, took a bullet, and went limp. Fickle air currents magnified the horror a hundred fold, errant gusts that pushed the unluckiest over the island's towering rim and onto the sharp outcroppings below.

Enemy bodies blown from defending vessels floated in the water. As the Flagstaff drew back from its last salvo, circling the battle scene, deck hands tossed rope lines to enemy survivors bobbing in the water. One after another opened his mouth and sank beneath the surface, suicide over surrender. But not all, Johnny Shepherd saw from his hideaway. A lone survivor grasped the line tossed to him and held on as four deck hands hoisted the dripping captive thirty feet to the deck.

Pickett had popped through a hatch from the lower decks. "Hey what the hell is this? Saving Japs?" he shouted over the chaos. "Thought we was here to kill the bastards, not rescue 'em. Figure that's what would happen if we was in the water."

Of the ship's 1300 crewmembers, only a few echoed Pickett's anger, as many inched forward for a closer look at the captive. "Yeah, whatta we doing, rescuing Japs?" yelled a gunner's mate, Garvin, from the crowd, which receded at the voice of a ship's officer, taking command of the moment. From another knot of rubberneckers, Davis, a Yeoman First Class who knew Johnny as "Shep", voiced a different sentiment. "You couple of tough guys better remember there are international rules on treatment of POWs."

The ship's brig had been empty at the battle's start. But within moments, it held the prisoner, the Japanese sailor minus his uniform but clothed in dry, insignia-free US Navy dungarees.

The Flagstaff's lone Marine, a Guadalcanal veteran, was posted as guard during the day.

At week's end, in the early a.m. hours, startling news passed through the warship's passages and battle stations that the Japanese sailor was dead, face down, halfway on his bunk, stabbed in the heart by a thin-bladed knife, with the brig's door of steel bars locked. An investigation by the Flagstaff's top brass was underway.

Below decks, Johnny felt the Flagstaff change course, circling to rejoin the convoy, withdrawing from its assault position and leaving it to Allied ground troops to retake the rock fortress from Japanese fighters dug in.

***

For Johnny Shepherd, the odyssey began months before under a searing Pacific sun as one by by one three men hopped from the well of the bobbing landing craft to the platform of the ladder leading up to the deck of the light cruiser, USS Flagstaff. Over the ship's rail catcalls rained down from old hands. "Hey, here comes new shark bait!"

"What's the matter landlubbers? Didn't you like the jungle juice?" They knew all about the potent coconut milk brew on New Guinea, staging area for replacement crew members fresh from the States.

"I'll bet somebody in this bunch has got a pygmy head to trade," a railbird shouted. I'll pay twenty-five bucks. Uncle Sam dollars."

A tall, rangy sailor, dressed in work dungarees, emerged from a hatchway. "I'm Eddie Redhorse," he said, grinning and pointing at the stenciled insignia on his right sleeve, a single chevron with a globe fixed over it, an electrician's insignia. "Screw those dirtbags. We got more than a thousand guys glad to pipe you aboard.

"Follow me below," Eddie added with a smirk, "and I'll show you the presidential suite."

Along their journey through the labyrinth of passageway, dungaree-clad sailors paused to scan the greenhorns. "You'll be sorry," cracked a shirtless sailor, with stubble poking through the grease on his face. Eddie, a Navajo, stopped at a crews' quarters aft in the ship. "This is it," Eddie said. "Home!. Bunks without mattresses are up for grabs." Johnny Shepherd picked a top bunk, a rectangle of canvas lashed to a supporting bar. Schlosser took the middle bunk and Dawson, senior at 27, chose the bottom bunk, easier to use.

At that moment the ship's PA system bellowed: "Now hear this. Electrician trainees, Dawson, Schlosser and Shepherd, lay to the electrical shop on the double."

The trio fumbled their way through passageways and compartments, opening and securing hatches. At length—there it was—the electrical shop, a cage-like setup, rimmed inside by long workbenches, and a cage within the cage, bristling with electric motors, armatures, electric parts and tools.

Once inside the cage-like room, a lieutenant in pressed khakis scanned the three up and down. "Well, you made it to the USS Flagstaff. I'm Lt. Bruce DeVere" His mouth turned down in exaggerated toughness, and the words came out stagey, contrived. He wasn't, they knew, regular Navy, but a banker, drafted from his hometown of Muncie, Indiana. "You new men," he went on, switching his gaze away from the assemblage of ten or so veteran sailors stiffly at attention, and then back to the new crew members, "will be working with my experienced men." He paused, "They'll teach you all you need to know. Goldbrick and you'll wish you'd joined the infantry. He turned to leave, uttering a curt "dismissed."

One of the regulars, rail-thin, almost as thin as Shep, with thick, brown hair combed straight back, sized up Shep, the kid of the new recruits, announcing, "I'm Earl Fletcher. Like the Lieutenant said, "I'll be your coach—until you can fly on your own, and the sooner the better."

"Shepherd, Johnny."

"Not much use for first name around here, but I use 'Fletch'." The rest of the electrical gang, except one, in contrast to Fletch's cold-faced way, shook hands and exchanged hometowns.

Eddie Redhorse called Tucson home, which put him closer to Flagstaff, namesake of the cruiser, than any of the group. Names attached themselves to towns and cities in predictable order. Trombetti from South Philly, McNeil from Jersey. Otto Herr from Pennsylvania Dutch country. Giannini, called G.I., from Baltimore's Little Italy. O'Reilly from Boston. Grossdecker from upstate New York. Pickett from Anniston, Alabama. And so it went.

***

That evening at chow, Shep's first meal aboard a fighting ship of the line, Jim Dawson folded his gawky frame onto the narrow bench next to Johnny in the mess hall. Both of their compartmented trays held tasteless gobs, Saturday's usual "stars and stripes"—the sailors' name for bacon and beans.

"I heard where we're heading," Dawson whispered, his hawk-like nose pointed straight ahead as though he wasn't talking to Shep, who knew his companion had finished law school, but not the bar.

"Okay, where's that?"

"Only the brass know. But it's Corregidor.

The Allies are aiming to shoot for recapture. We'll support a parachute landing there. With Dugout Doug on the Nashville standing by."

"Mac Arthur? Corregidor? How do you know? Johnny Shepherd whispered.

"Heard it from the cook. Like the brass, the cooks always know."

Shep struggled to recall details from the newsreels. Wasn't General Mac Arthur in charge at Bataan, where the Japanese captured thousands of prisoners, then marched them to Manilla, killing thousands? They called it the 'Death March.' That's what the newsreels said."

Shep looked at Dawson, older, maybe wiser. "That thing about Dugout Dug... where'd it come from?"

Jim Dawson, scowling, said, "It's after he retreated to Corregidor in '42, then later took off for Australia with the President of the Philippines. Just before the Corregidor allied holdout surrendered. Remember that boast, 'I shall return?' That was for reporters after he reached Australia, where he was supposed to organize the invasion of Japan. But captured prisoners in Philippine prison camps came up with the "Dugout Doug" nickname. I heard there's two guys on our ship, one, Garvin, a gunner's mate, and 'Dusty' Rhodes, a psycho from Frisco, had brothers in that march."

"Anyway, two years later and Corregidor's our target—here we are 'returning.' The Japanese holed up will be shooting—at us. If we take a hit, we'd better figure out fast how to keep this ship afloat and moving."

***

Fletcher, Shep's coach from day one, approached the world with narrow-eyed defiance. He harbored an uncanny knack for diagnosing mysterious electrical failures and fixing them in short order. The skill rewarded him with two stripes of a second class petty officer, bucking for first class, and, probably, warrant officer. Once when he left his wallet and a red-handled foreign knife with different sized blades and tools in the electrician's cage, Shep chased him down to return them but before he caught up the contents slipped out, and, in picking them up, he noticed a Seattle locksmith's certificate made out to a Samuel Morris. Fletcher grabbed the left-behind items with a frown.

The Flagstaff had two engine rooms, fore and aft, housing massive steam turbines. Opposite stood the electrical switchboards, seven feet high and maybe ten feet wide, crammed with dials for recording the ebb and flow of power running the vessel's hundreds of motors. From the overhead, trumpet-like blowers rushed life-giving air from topside decks to the engine room's Hades-hot bowels.

A week after Shep had reported aboard Fletcher led him to the forward engine room. "You'll be spending a lot of time here," he shouted over the blowers' roar.

"It's hot down here."

He snickered. "This is just a warmup. Wait till we get underway."

"When's that?" Shep asked.

"Today, 1500 hours."

"Where to?"

"Better not to worry your head, but we'll be passing the Solomon Islands. Your job is to learn the switchboard. And stay under the blowers." He smirked. "You'll fry if you don't. Over by the turbine it can nudge 150."

Fletcher stood up. His hands moved like a concert pianist's over the bank of switches and circuit breakers as he shouted, "Overloads can trip these. Sometimes you'll have to flick them back on fast. If you start to lose voltage, you'll have to figure where to cut juice to conserve power. Don't screwup and cut current to the topside guns."

Shep's stomach flipped. Flagstaff's own crew could get killed by his mistake. Fletcher picked up on his fear. "You'll get it, junior. You got to." He snickered. "And don't borrow my tools—they're special made. And while you're working it all out, don't turn your back on that sonofabitch McNeil." Shep wondered if McNeil could out nasty Fletcher.

Back in the electrical shop, O'Reilly turned his beet-red face to Shep. "So, babe, how do you like being Flagshafted so far?" he said, strapping a tool kit on. Nobody laughed at the Flagstaff joke, rust-covered by now.

"Suits me, okay," Shep said. "Better than New Guinea and scorpions."

Grossdecker, who'd been at Pearl Harbor Dec. 7, '41, chimed in: "Oh yeah, how about when the Nips start dropping 500 pounders down the stack? Just watch me if I ever get my hands one one of those slant-eyed sneak attackers."

Everybody knew as a civilian Pickett had been in a bar fight and killed a black guy, but got off on self defense. Before he picked up his gear to leave, he said to Shep, "Big deal. Smart ass because you made electrician's school."

Eddie lingered and pulled Shep aside. "Here's the best info you're gonna get.

Everything that happens in the electrical gang gets back to DeVere. We don't know how or why, but it does."

***

With the Corregidor engagement three days behind and fading, Shep watched the Flagstaff ease into formation with a convoy of vessels, destroyers and carriers, underway westward zigzagging at the same speed and probing the air with radar and the deep sea with sonar fingers, feeling for torpedoes.

It took three days until a matter-of-fact announcement over the 1MC loudspeakers said the dead POW would be buried at sea in full uniform.

Pickett ranted, "Now ain't that just ducky. Guess if he was alive, we give him a medal." Grossdecker confined his displeasure to frowns and grunts.

Shep met Jim Dawson in the passageway coming from a repair job in the aft engine room.

"How do you figure it?" Jim, "We're not getting debriefed on what happened in the brig?"

"My guess is someone's taking the easy way out."

"So we got maybe a murderer on board. You're a lawyer. Don't they have to do something?"

"Far as I know it's up to the Captain. But there's those Geneva Convention rules protecting enemy combatants."

Abruptly, the weather turned nasty. The Flagstaff began rolling,. Then waves, kicked up by the rising wind, tipped the cruiser to port and starboard, tilting sailors on deck precariously close to the roiling water. Clutching a gun mount. Shep tasted the wind-whipped spray. Monsoon rains fell like gray curtains. Over the howling wind a deck officer announced over the 1MC public address system, "All hands below! This is a typhoon! Wind is force six. Barometer 29.10 and falling."

A wave rising like a phantom mountain crashed over the ship's bow. Half a day the storm raged. Below decks men clutched their stomachs and heaved as they clung to precarious perches. When the wind slacked, all vessels in the flotilla were afloat.

The announcement came for all hands to re-stow fallen gear back on shelves and tables. Electrical damage to Flagstaff from port-to-starboard 30-degree rolling was minimal, but loose wires dangled like spaghetti. Shep found himself wrestling solo with a high-ampere galley motor in which he installed contact brushes, methodically taped up the leads, tested the motor and congratulated himself on a job well done.

Or so he thought. Next day scuttlebutt had DeVere following up with damage-control, finding things ship shape again, except the taping of a particular galley motor. It had been clumsy. Johnny's work. Johnny Shepherd had become his special target.

On the fourth day out, the bridge rescheduled the sea burial, but at the electrical shop McNeil suddenly swung through the hatchway. Anger contorted his face. "Okay, big trouble here," he shouted to five of us cleaning the metal deck with carbon tetrachloride. "There's three hundred bucks missing from my locker!"

"Maybe you mislaid it," Shep said, groping for a way to curb the rage.

"Yeah," Otto Herr chimed in. "That could happen."

"Don't give me that bull," McNeil snapped.

"It was a break-in?" Schlosser wondered.

McNeil's dour face twisted with new anger. "My locker was locked. I'm reporting it to DeVere. There's a lock picker around here. All you scabs know what happens to thieves."

***

Most of the ship's company watched without emotion as a topside contingent prepared to slip the body over the side. But another loudspeaker announcement interrupted: "Now hear this, the burial service is postponed until further notice." The electrical gang had watched and waited but as Shep lingered on deck, he tried to recall who'd boycotted the burial service. Pickett for sure. Probably Grossdecker. AWOL, Shep realized, were two seaman, Garvin and Rhodes, who'd lost brothers on the Death March.

***

Now destroyers, other cruisers, and carriers dotted a calm sea, beginning to obey identical orders for speed and course settings. Slowly, the flotilla circled in the bright, blue water waiting for something—something deck hands weren't privileged to know. Shep slithered into the shade under a gun mount to escape the relentless sun. Moments later, Jim Dawson on his back inched toward Shep, until they rested their heads on a coiled fire hose.

"Listen to this," Dawson said. "I talked to that Marine guard, who was posted during daylight hours by the brig to keep the ugly few at a distance. Get this: The Jap once lived in Seattle, talks English just like you and me. Lived there—this was '41— until he was slapped into one of those prison camps.

"After he was locked in our brig, the guard reported, he watched that parade of gawkers. Now listen. At one point the Jap recognized one of the gawkers, and called out, 'Sam, it's me, Ken Hisao'." But whoever Sam was spun and left without a word."

"Somebody he knew from back in the States?"

"Could be. The Marine doesn't know squat about Navy insignia, only noted two chevrons on the exiting gawker's sleeve."

"Second class Petty Officer, then," Shep confirmed. "Anything else?"

"Well, they had retrieved his ID papers, dried them out. The prisoner also said he'd been in locksmith school with 'Sam' but couldn't remember his last name, only that he'd run into trouble with the law."

"How did our prisoner end up in the Japanese Navy?"

"Somehow an enemy submarine crew smuggled him out of the camp and back to

Japan. He was one of those Japanese Americans, a prime source to look for US war plans."

"Sort of forced to spy?"

"Right."

Shep turned toward Jim Dawson. "If we only knew what happened in the officer's wardroom when they talked about the prisoner's fate...."

"Dangerous territory, lad. Keep me out of your snooping. By the way, I heard from Giannini, once a psychiatric social worker, why DeVere second-guesses you. He's embarrassed; his son in Muncie is a conscientious objector, so he takes it out on you, the closest kid."

"Kind of nutty. Anyway, somebody must have kept a record of the wardroom talk."

"Maybe that First Class Yeoman typist and short hand guy—Davis, I think."

Shep sat up, bumping his head. "Hey, I know him. We've chewed the fat about West Virginia. We both lived about ten miles apart. I'll talk to him."

***

When Shep found an out-of-the-way corner to confer, Davis fidgeted nervously, reluctant to talk.

"It's just between you and me now."

"Okay, but I could lose a stripe if this gets out. Still, I don't like what happened either."

"So?"

"Well, the meeting was the Captain, and two other gold braiders," Davis said, casting his eyes around. Truth is, they couldn't figure out what happened to the prisoner. The brig was locked when the mess attendant delivered his chow. The Marine, who had just come back on duty, didn't have a key and the brig door was locked. The First Looey with the key, opened the door and found the Jap dead. Later, they called in a Pharmacist Mate to confirm a three and a half inch blade inflicted the wound to the body, now packed in ice from the ship's reefer."

"So the stabber got in," Shep said.

"Or the prisoner killed himself, and threw the knife overboard."

"Now listen to this Jim," Shep said. "At first I figured Pickett. Wouldn't put anything past him. Grossdecker sounded plenty mad ."

"You better watch out for those those Death March brothers, Garvin and that psycho, Rhodes."

"Yeah, sure, but listen to this. What if I say I think—and I can't believe it myself— I may know who that 'Sam' was." Shep paused. "Let's get Jim Dawson. He went to law school."

Later, the three, including a nervous Dawson, huddled out of view near the ship's bow. Johnny Shepherd recounted Yeoman Davis's account of the wardroom discussion. "Jim, you learned from the Marine that the prisoner went to locksmith school with a guy named Sam , who the prisoner recognized for an instant in the gawker parade.

"You know who else is a locksmith? A guy named 'Fletch'."

"I'm not sure I want to think what I think you're thinking."

"And think about another lock that was picked—the one on McNeil's locker when his three hundred bucks was stolen."

"This is all circumstantial," Dawson protested.

"What if I say I spotted a card in Fletcher's wallet with the name Samuel Morrison, a certified locksmith? He also owns a funny kind of foreign knife with a red handle."

Jim Dawson frowned in thought. "Maybe he faked his ID, switched to Fletcher so he could join the Navy. Remember, the Japanese prisoner mentioned 'Sam's' trouble with the law back home in Seattle."

"But why kill the prisoner?" Davis asked.

Dawson said, "I get it. Fletcher—really Sam —was bucking for First Class. If faking his name to join the Navy got out, he'd be knocked off the ladder, maybe out of the service."

"So what now? Shep ask. "We've got to tell someone."

"You've got to tell someone," Dawson said. "The First Lieutenant, the ship's administrative officer, Robert Travers. He was the only one suggesting they should pursue the killer. With the Captain's okay, he could have Fletcher's belongings searched. But Johnny, for your sake, I hope you're right. Or this could be big trouble. And you'd better let DeVere in on this."

***

As Lt. Travers listened to Shep's story, anxiety, marked his face, knowing he was caught between duty and uncertainty. With the Marine Guard and two deck officers, Travers carried out the search with Fletcher detained on deck.

At first nothing, but a second sweep, including a look inside spit-and-polish shoes stashed at the bottom of Fletcher's seabag, produced a thin, curved, metal rod resembling a dentist's tool and red-handled knife with a blade that flipped in and out, but with no obvious

117

blood. So Fletcher/Morrison was too cocky and possessive to deep six the knife and his favorite lock-picking instrument, which he may have used to pick McNeil's locker, and maybe even the brig's lock.

Sewed neatly in the mattress was three hundred in tens, each marked with a dot of ink, a symbol inscribed by a paranoid McNeil each time he exchanged his fives and ones for tens, as the ship's purser attested.

What really jolted the electrical gang was news of a diary with reports on each member Fletch had sent to DeVere, proving Fletch was the secret snitch all along—even confirming that DeVere had promised Fletch a First Class rank in exchange for inside dirt. Now DeVere was branded with a real embarrassment and maybe loss of his commission.

Whoever stabbed the prisoner probably lured him near the bars to look like somebody reached in from outside. But there was a spanner in the works. Later, the prisoner, not quite dead, apparently pulled himself to the bunk. The trail of blood beneath showed he was not close enough to the bars to take an outside thrust. Someone had entered the brig. Worse for Fletcher, a machinist mate reported seeing

Fletch on the brig's deck around 3 in the morning.

Shep told Jim Dawson, "With Lt. Traver's report, the Captain instructed a Radioman to contact Navy officials in Seattle and check out the dual backgrounds of Earl Fletcher and Samuel Morrison. The word came back detailing locksmith Samuel Morrison's checkered civilian career."

* * *

"Fletch," still in full denial of murder, glowered back from the launch, idling in the water at the bottom of the ladder leading down from the Flagstaff's main deck. Under escort, facing a court-martial, he was headed for a battleship ordered to Pearl for repairs. The body of the dead prisoner would follow by air as evidence.

"Whatever else happens," said Lieutenant Travers, standing next to Shep, "Fletcher will get maximum punishment for fraudulent enlistment."

Earlier, Shep had discovered the prisoner's name, Hisao, meant "long-lived man" in Japanese.

Watching the departure, Johnny Shepherd felt behind him the seething hate of Pickett and half a dozen others, a small, angry minority of the Flagstaff's 1,300 seamen, who knew, in the chaos of war, something had gone right.

Tourada À Corda

Howard B. Carron

We all stood there as he placed a rope around the leg and hoisted him into the air about a foot off the ground. Two men grasped his head and a third stepped forward and with a lightning slash exposed the jugular; a second stroke and a fountain of steamy blood gushed out to be caught in a large tub placed just below the head. The shrill scream, which filled the small room, stopped abruptly as the body went limp and only an occasional twitch remained. We stood there in awe of this ritual execution, performed with swift and unerring accuracy, by our host.

The pig was left to drain further, the blood was mixed with vinegar to help it coagulate, turned into a large cauldron and brought slowly to a boil.

Working with the efficiency of a forensic pathologist the farmer opened the pig from the neck down to the navel with deft strokes from a sharp knife and the innards spilled out into yet another bucket. The heart, liver, kidneys and intestines were gently removed and placed aside.

The area around the genitals was very carefully cut to prevent fouling the meat with any toxic material and the bladder was removed and placed in a pan of water to be cleaned and later given to the children to be used as a balloon!

Next the animal was lowered and carried outside of the small "killing room" to the yard where a fire was quickly bringing a 55 gallon drum (which had been split in half and filled with water) to a boil. The pig was lifted and placed into the boiling water of the half drum for a minute or two and then placed on a long wooden table. Taking a device shaped like half of a metal ball with a handle, this scraper was used in a circular motion to remove all the hair from the skin.

The process of dipping and scraping continued until all the hair was removed. Starting just below the head a series of powerful blows delivered with a hand axe split the animal into two parts along the backbone. A few more blows and the head was removed. The rest of the pig was dismembered into large portions, the feet removed and the nails pulled out with pliers. The fat surrounding the kidney, the caul, was reserved for use in making pie crusts after it was rendered, all extra back fat was put in another pot to be rendered, belly removed for bacon and the tongue cleaned and put aside for a special meal (*Lengua*) with the rest of the head ground up for a concoction not unlike our Philadelphia scrapple. The intestine was cleaned and put aside to be used for sausage casing.

A scimitar shaped knife was used to separate the back fat from the skin efficiently and the skin was cut up into small pieces, boiled and fried to make another delicacy. As one of my farmer friends put it, "they use everything but the squeal."

The killing of this rather large pig was our introduction to the realities of life on the island of Terceira, Azores. Most of us had been city dwellers and the closest we had ever come to a pig was the selection of pork chops, neatly wrapped, in the BX Commissary or our local butcher shop back home.

The Azores are a group of nine Portuguese islands, discovered about 1427, in the Atlantic Ocean about 740 miles northwest of southern Portugal. Terceira, which means third (not the size but the order of discovery), is 18 miles long and 10 miles wide. Winemaking and agriculture are the mainstays of the population. There are three main villages; Angra de Heroisima, Praia de Vittorio and Lajes.

I was a civilian employee working as a communications specialist for the schools, educating the dependents of the U.S. Military. The Air Force Base at Lajes Field, basically a re-fueling stop for aircraft (United States., Portuguese, Iranian, English, Israeli, etc.), was commanded by the Navy with an Army detachment responsible for patrolling the waters in a couple of World War II vintage PT boats. During World War II Lajes was an important anti-submarine base.

Within a couple of months we found ourselves living in a farmhouse, having moved up from a tiny apartment in Praia de Vittorio. I became "El Professor" to the local inhabitants as I struggled with the mechanics of the Portuguese language and practiced on everyone. Fortunately for me, I had considerable experience in first aid and woodworking, a strange combination of skills which endeared me to the locals as I helped them repair their farming equipment with my electric tools (powered by a generator in the back of my truck) and treating various cuts and bruises for my neighbors who couldn't or wouldn't go to the local doctor. At any rate, life was good!

We acquired four horses and spent much time exploring this quaint environment time-locked into the 18th century. I would even pack my golf clubs on the back of my horse and trot off through the fog, on the cobblestone streets, to the moon-scaped golf course. Because of the ever-present fog, finding and hitting the golf ball was always a challenge.

Shana, a student at the High School, offered to teach our family how to ride horses and she became a member of our family. She was the stepdaughter of a Navy corpsman and the woman who was the charge desk assistant at the base library. Flaming red hair, fair skin, pale green eyes and a band of freckles across her nose accompanied a personality and demeanor beyond her 18 years of age. We became friends (as close as my professional responsibilities would allow) and my wife and daughters adored her.

Shana knew all about animals and raised her own pig, which she had dubbed Arnold. Lori, my youngest daughter had a pet goat and would always ask Shana questions about her "Nanny". This friendship was put to the supreme test when Shana's pig was dispatched to the freezer. Coming from a farming background this was a natural chain of events for Shana but when she offered my daughter Lori a piece of "Arnold" it was a trying time. Lori swore that her "Nanny" would never meet that fate even though *cabrito* (goat roasted with wine, garlic, onion and olive oil) was a staple food on the island.

Lori and Melody (my oldest daughter) tried their hand at taming the landlord's dog "Cao" which translates to "dog" in Portuguese. He was a matted, miserable animal who spent his life tied up near the outhouse in the backyard. Animals are not pets in this community and as long as he did his job of guarding the house he was fed. The girls undertook to clean and groom him and Senor Coehlo, the landlord, just shook his head but didn't interfere.

Since we lived on a farm we tried our hand at planting potatoes, corn, tomatoes, onions, and at my insistence, some Chinese cabbage. The local farmers had never seen this plant although their cabbage, *repollo*, was a staple of their diet. I allowed some of the Chinese cabbage plants to go to seed and many of our neighbors planted some finding it a tasty alternative to *repollo*. Repollo is used in many recipes including a marvelous soup concoction called *sopa verde* (green soup).

126

About the middle of the semester, sometime in early December, it became a little too chilly for horseback riding but Shana continued to visit. One day she stopped by my office to ask for help on a research project, wearing, not her usual jeans and blouse but a long, shapeless shift. I was kidding her about the outfit and asked if she had a bonnet to go with it. She laughed and shook her head and then I really put my foot in my mouth.

"The only ladies I ever see wearing that kind of outfit are either (a) in the movies, (b) cleaning house or (c) pregnant," I said and chuckled.

Sitting down on the edge of a chair by my desk she said, "try (c)."

I felt like a complete jerk and my usual repartee deserted me. After taking a moment to absorb this I blurted out, "who, why."

"I can't tell you who but the why part is easy. I was raped."

"Shana, why didn't you report this to the Military Police? They could have locked up this creep. You can't let him get away with this."

Slowly shaking her head, tears running down her cheeks she said very quietly "No one would believe me."

127

More questioning on my part elicited no further information and after telling me not to worry that she would take care of it, she left. I guess I sat there for the next hour considering what I would do if this were my daughter. Slowly my shock segued into a mounting anger. This military community was very small and insular and I knew, with some judicious probing, I might come up with some information but I would need Shana's cooperation once I had some leads.

I had a good friend in the legal office, 1st Lt. John Cabrielli, the school liaison officer. I called him and using general details asked him to check on any suspicious sex related or family abuse activity with the Military Police. He promised to check and call me back.

A couple of days later John called and told me that there was not even a murmur of any reports of unwanted sexual activity. I tried to figure out a way to get some information from my High School student assistants.

Shana's brother, Raymond, did odds and ends of electrical and electronic repairs for me. Another redhead, he had an unsavory reputation dealing with authority, especially with his step-father. His work for me was excellent but he was extremely reserved in the workshop. The other assistants were only juniors and would not be privy to any information about the seniors, a very small, closely knit and elite group.

The problem was further complicated by the physical layout of the base. Perched close to the top of the area known as Santa Rita hill there wasn't a road that did not go up or down. In fact, the local bus, a wheezing old Mercedes-Benz, just barely made the trip up the 45-degree hill and most of the time passengers jumped off to lighten the load so the bus could make it. There was a long, low building connecting the Elementary School with the Junior High School and then the music room and shop and my area between that and the High School. Except for lunchtime activities, band and the library there was little interaction between the grades.

After two more days of probing with the students the only lead I had was Raymond, Shana's brother. Before tackling him I decided to check with the school counselor to see if she knew of anything concerning Shana and Raymond and their family situation. Perhaps I might find a way to get through to them.

Davina Carol's office was festooned with artifacts from around the island; baskets, cow bells, old clocks, a lobster trap and photographs of just about every Festa, (local block parties), held during the year. It was really a comfortable place for kids and adults alike and her disposition was always sunny and helpful.

That day Davina was wearing an orchid jumpsuit. Her full figure was shown to good advantage by her carefully chosen outfit. Her hair was wrapped in a Moroccan turban from her last vacation, with her collection of bangles and beads very much in evidence. After five minutes of a general sharing of recent activities and an animated discussion of her plans for the upcoming winter break, we got down to business. While it is unprofessional to share intimate details of students, we are, as educators, entitled to information, which would give us insight into their behavior. This was, of course, on a "need to know" basis.

Without mentioning Shana I explained that I was concerned with Raymond's withdrawn and often brooding behavior.

Her reply, *"Nao faz mal,"* the local equivalent of no problem was followed by her removal of a file from her cabinet. Since I wasn't entitled to all of its contents she looked it over carefully and then gave me an outline of events based upon my inquiry. Raymond had a higher than average I.Q., a proclivity for electronics, an average school record (too low for his I.Q.) and a series of attitude problems most likely generated by his stepfather's drinking and verbally abusive behavior. His preoccupation with family problems was a likely cause for his lack of attentiveness in class. The father had been in counseling a few times for alcoholism but there were no recent incidents reported. It seemed he had that problem under control. As far as any family abuse or domestic violence there were no recent reports but that may be because the military does not intervene in household problems unless they interfere with military member's job.

Davina said, "The military is not too big on family counseling just yet. I met Dorothy Curtis at the Base Library and once for a conference about Raymond. She is a petite and very timid woman. Of Portuguese extraction, dark hair and olive complexion, probably attractive at one time, she seemed overwhelmed by the family relationship. She told me she met her second husband when he was stationed in Rhode Island, at the NCO club where she worked after her first husband was killed in the Vietnam conflict.

Stan Curtis was much more introverted than her first husband, a light-hearted, red-haired, Irishman. With two children to raise, she felt marriage was a sensible move. I guess she believes that you do what you have to do to survive."

Davina also pointed out that Dorothy spoke Portuguese which made her invaluable in her job when dealing with local vendors and workers.

After leaving Davina's office I stopped by the General Shop to speak with Jerry Johns, the instructor, who often was the recipient of community gossip from the students. He told me that he had overheard some of the girls discussing Raymond's father because he had been trying to make some moves on a couple of senior girls and that they were afraid for Shana.

I felt a cold chill settling in my stomach at the possible implications of this information. I had to talk to Raymond who was in my center repairing some damaged phonographs for the elementary school.

As I approached the repair area I heard some shouting and recognizing Raymond's voice opened the door quietly. Nose to nose, a Navy Corpsman and Raymond were arguing.

"You bastard," Raymond hissed through

clenched teeth, "how could you, your own kid!"

They both turned around as soon as they realized they were not alone and the Corpsman brushed past me into the corridor.

"What was that all about," I said, approaching the workbench. "Who was that?"

"My stepfather," Raymond spat out as tears filled his eyes and he turned away from me and tried to change the subject.

"These are ready to go," he said in a voice quivering with anger.

"Forget about the phonographs. What is going on?"

"I don't want to talk about it," he muttered.

"Look Raymond, I talked with Shana and she told me she had been attacked. I want to help. You know you can trust me."

"I know, Mr. Carlton. You've always been up front with me but this is really bad."

"How bad?"

Clenching his hands in front of him he took a deep breath and told me that his stepfather had forced himself on Shana and was responsible for her being pregnant. His mother didn't know, and he and Shana were planning on going back to Rhode Island, "Space A," during the Winter Recess and have it taken care of.

Since Shana didn't report it right away it would be hard to prove. We both knew that the military solution would be to transfer his stepfather and the likelihood of his being prosecuted was slight. On top of that, in such a small community, the effect on Shana and his mother would be devastating. We left it at that, at least for the present.

I talked with 1st Lt. Cabrielli and posed the scenario, without mentioning names and he confirmed what Raymond and I had already decided; it would be next to impossible to prosecute under the circumstances I had described.

Terceira is, as I mentioned, a rather small island, but this did not deter the inhabitants from having innumerable festivals and one of those was running the bulls down the main street from Lajes to Praia de Vittorio. Two weeks before Christmas the cobblestone streets were lined with villagers and guests from the military installation. The local band (every village, no matter how small, had a band) was playing their rendition of bullfight music, slightly off-key but loud and exuberant. Every veranda, porch and wall that lined the street was crowded with people.

134

Terceira is well known for their *tourada à corda* or bullfight with a bull tethered by a rope, the *corda*. While other islands such as Sao Jorge may have a running of the bulls occasionally you will not find this particular spectacle anywhere else . The bull is kept in a wooden box and before he is let loose a small rocket is launched which provides a loud noise. This is a signal indicating that a bull is on the street and the game is ready to begin.

The bull is let loose with a very long rope around its neck, usually at the main road in a small village. The bull is guided by a group of six to eight men who try to keep the bull away from non-welcoming places. However, pretty much free reign is given to the bull when confined to the streets and the plaza where the event is to take place. The whole idea is to have the local young men try to get as close to the bull as they dare without getting gored, and teasing the bull who becomes quite frenzied.

While the game is often amusing and the young men do it to impress the local girls, it is very dangerous. Not all succeed in this, and some are seriously injured. Every year there are fatal casualties as a result of this primitive form of sport. This year there were to be three bulls in the *tourada à corda,*

As I moved towards the center of town I noticed Stan Curtis, dressed in Navy whites, along with two of his buddies, seated at an outside café table. On an impulse I walked over and as I approached a flicker of recognition flashed in his eyes.

"Hey, you're the guy that Raymond helps out in school, right? Sit down and have a drink."

They had a bottle of the local red wine in front of them but I asked for a glass of Esmeralda Oporto, brought in from Portugal.

" What kind of drink is that?" Curtis asked

"One of the finest Port wines you'll find anywhere in the world."

"Yeah, well this wine, at 11 cents a bottle, suits us fine, even if it is a little weak."

Inwardly I wanted to hit him over the head with the bottle but called the proprietor over instead.

"Senhor, Um garrafa de Aguadent, por favor." The carafe arrived quickly and was presented with a broad smile.

"Mr. Curtis, you want a real drink. Try this one. It's Aguadent, Portuguese 'White Lightning,' but a lot smoother."

Curtis knocked back the drink. His eyes watered and his nostrils flared but in keeping

136

with his macho image he said, "Not bad."
Watching his reaction the other two sailors
carefully sipped their drinks. I'm not sure how
much wine he had previously but he put away
four or five more shots of the Aguadent. By this
time the festa was in full swing and I left to join
the crowd alongside the road.

Prior to the releasing of the bulls, the plaza
was crowded with people as pitchers of young
red wine were passed around along with
Masasafada, a golden round bread made with
fresh eggs and wild honey and slathered with
locally produced creamy butter. By the time the
villagers and guests took their places they were
loose and happy.

Part of the ritual was, of course, for the
young men to run before the bulls and jump up
on the wall at the last minute, out of harms way.
A sort of "rite of passage," with some element of
danger, but the agile runners were quite adept at
this sport.

As the bulls thundered down the
cobblestones amid the shouts of encouragement
from the crowd, the nimble runners easily
outdistanced the bulls thanks to the restraint of
the rope. The bulls were fast approaching the
fountain in the center of the plaza when three
men dressed in navy whites, three sheets to the

wind, jumped down and started to run with the villagers.

Two of them quickly thought better of the idea and jumped out of the way, scrambling up the wall, into the crowd amid rousing cheers and cries of *receoso* (afraid). The third one ran a zigzag course, the effects of the local wine quite obvious

The bulls, lathered in sweat, white foamy spittle spraying around them, nostrils flared and eyes white with fear, thundered towards him. The eight men holding the rope were unable to slow the lead bull. He misjudged the distance to the nearest wall. As he swung one leg over the wall one of the bulls swerved toward him and with a vicious swipe of his horns impaled him in the groin, tossing him into the crowd.

Suddenly it was quiet, except for the sound of the bulls' hooves on the cobblestones. Many of the older ladies, dressed in their customary black mourning garments, grasped their rosary beads and crossed themselves.

The bulls ran past the plaza and were driven around the fountain and then herded into a nearby open field. The crowd surged towards the stricken man and then parted as I pushed my way to the thrashing figure on the ground. The crowd of villagers looked at me expectantly because of my reputation as a first aid "expert"

Looking down I saw Stan Curtis, Shana and Raymond's stepfather, hands grasping his bloody crotch, writhing on the ground. All I could do was cover him with a blanket supplied by one of the villagers and wait for help.

An ambulance from the base arrived shortly thereafter and that was the last we saw of Stan Curtis. He was air evacuated to Bethesda Naval Hospital.

As a dependent wife Dorothy couldn't remain on Terceira without command sponsorship so she returned to Rhode Island to join her children. Shana wrote a couple of months later to tell me that everything had worked out for the best, her step-father didn't make it, succumbing to shock and loss of blood. She and her family were doing well. I wondered how much responsibility I should assume for his accident but then I remembered my favorite philosopher, Heraclitus: *"A man's character is his fate."*

One More Mission

Brendan DuBois

My first real shock of the day was going down the main access road to McIntosh Air Force Base—oops, now called McIntosh International Tradeport since the base closed a decade or so ago—to the place where the main gate used to be. Back when I was in the Air Force, there were smartly dressed and well-armed Air Police with blue berets and white scarves, checking every vehicle coming in. There had also been a visitor's building to the right, to process those people coming in to visit or make deliveries to families living on base, but that building was now a Greyhound bus station.

There were other changes as well. Absent were the stone and brass monuments to the 509th Bombardment Wing and the 157th Refueling Wing, which had once been stationed here, and the large billboard with the Strategic Air Command emblem and its motto, "Peace is our Profession."

The monuments were gone. The sign was gone. Instead, there was a billboard advertising prime business properties inside the former SAC base.

And one more shock as well, as I went down the road. There had once been three aircraft stationed by the gate, as a tourist attraction and a memorial to those who had flown them: a B-29 Boeing Superfortress, a prop-driven KC-97 Stratotanker refueling aircraft, and a B-52 Boeing Stratofortress. All had departed with the base closure, leaving behind just lots of memories.

Most of them good, but one particular one, not so good.

Which was why I was here today.

***

I drove around the old base roads for a while, seeing the one-story brick buildings that used to house the PX, the base movie theater, the different buildings for the various squadrons that had supported the air base. They had all been converted to other things: a shoe shop, a couple of restaurants and a number of office buildings for a variety of hi-tech outfits. But on some of the older brick buildings, you could still make out the shadows of the metal letters that had been installed there, marking in military fashion what had been what.

Another surprise: along the roads when I had been stationed here there had been yellow pylons, with blue lights on top, with stenciled signs that said if the blue lights started flashing, you were supposed to pull over and let official traffic scream by, because that meant an alert had been called.

Those were gone as well.

But the airstrip—one of the largest in the Northeast and an alternative emergency landing spot for the space shuttle—remained, and there were a number of civilian aircraft parked off the apron at one end, but I didn't care about those aircraft. Nope, I was going to the other end of the runway, and there, I found what I had been looking for.

My old aircraft, KC-135 Stratotankers, were lined up near four large hangers. This part of the runway was sealed off by a high chain link fence topped by barbed-wire, and the sight of that and a small guard shack made me smile. The Air Force had left this base many years ago, but an Air National Guard unit was still here.

I pulled my rental car over to the side and got up, walking to the fence. I looked at the old tankers—military versions of the old Boeing 707—and caught a scent of JP-4 jet fuel. My word, the memories that came through me when I detected that familiar odor.

Memories of refueling missions, traveling over the Atlantic and boring holes in the sky, refueling aircraft heading over to Europe, and missions to the Middle East and Asia as well. I almost laughed, as my chin actually started throbbing, recalling all the times I was flat on my belly in the rear of tankers just like those out there, control stick in hand, chin resting on a padded cushion that seemed designed to make your chin ache, looking down at the thirsty aircraft, rising up to greet you, the boom extending out to start refueling, at a rate of 6,500 gallons per minute and....

"Sir? You need anything?"

I turned and two Air National Guardsmen were standing outside of a Ford pickup truck, looking over at me, wearing zippered light green flightsuits. It looked like they were heading into the area where the tankers were parked.

I raised a hand in greeting. "Nope, doing fine. Just looking and remembering, that's all."

One guardsman got back into the truck, but the other one, smiling, came over to me. He seemed to be in his mid-30s, tanned and fit, with short black hair flecked a bit with white. He said,

"Did you used to fly on those?"

"That I did. A lot of time, flat on my belly."

His smile widened. "Boomer, right?"

"Right," I said. "An expert at passing gas."

That brought a laugh and he stood next to me, as a KC-135 slowly taxied out and made its way to the main runway. The sound of the old Pratt & Whitney jet engines came to us and my, there was no other sound in the world like it. "Good old birds, aren't they," the guardsman said.

"True," I said. "God, when I was flying them, they were already older than the crew. Nowadays, they must be older than your father, am I right?"

He folded his arms and said, "One of these days, we're promised replacements."

"Sure," I said. "One of these days. I won't hold my breath if you don't."

We both watched as the refueling aircraft paused at the end of the runway, turned around, and waited. The engines revved up and then it started moving, faster and faster, and then delicately—like an old ballerina, still wanting to show off her skills—the Boeing aircraft lifted up and moved off to the east. Something tight tingled in my chest and I said, "Hard to believe,

144

they're still flying... hell, I think the last one came off the production line back in 1965."

"They're vital aircraft," the guardsmen said. "Can't have an Air Force with reach without an airborne gas station... but I don't have to tell you that."

"Nope."

We watched as the aircraft shrank out to the distance, and then a horn honked. The guardsmen said, "Sorry, gotta go." He stuck out his hand, which I shook.

"Thanks for your service," he said.

"No, thank you," I replied. "That was my full-time job, back in the day. You guys... you gotta squeeze in your flying time with your civilian life. Sometimes that can be a real chore."

He shrugged. "We all got jobs to do."

I nodded, thinking of why I had come here. "Sure. We all do."

***

I drove around the base for just a few minutes more, saw the acres of land where base housing used to be. Now there was nothing but rough fields, and I remember a story I had read, years ago, when the air base had been closed down. Local realtors and taxpayer groups didn't want all the base housing to come on the market

145

at once, for fear of depressing property values and tax revenues... and plus, most of the base housing wasn't up to current building codes. That last statement made me laugh out loud when I had read it. The housing was good enough to house military dependents when the base was open, but when the base was closed, the housing was quickly found to be sub-standard.

An old story about a society's values... and one I was going to revisit, before I was done for the day.

***

Outside of the old base I made a turn and went to a familiar part of town. There it was, just as I had remembered it: "Sonny and Sal's Famous Pizza!" But just like the air base itself, the pizza joint had changed a lot. Back when I was stationed here, it was a little place, built in a converted gas station. Now, it had expanded with two additions on either side of the old gas station, and the parking lot was nearly full. And when it had first opened up, it seemed like it was only weeks away from closing because business was so poor and the parking lot was almost always empty.

And I remembered what a fellow sergeant

had said to me, years ago: "That pizza place... it's a miracle it hasn't gone under yet. It's like they have some rich friends, keeping them afloat, month after month."

I parked my car, got out and walked in. *Yeah*, I thought. *Rich friends. Or not-so-rich neighbors.*

***

Inside the place was bustling and there was rock music playing softly on a jukebox, and it looked like most of the people worked at the old base, either in one of the civilian companies or at the Air National Guard wing, for there were a few uniformed folks scattered around. I had two slices of plain pizza and a Coke, and then I asked the waitress if I could see one of the owners, that it was very important to talk to him.

She said, "It's gonna have to be Sonny. Sal's in Boston today."

"That's fine," I said, and in a few minutes, I was in a back office, sitting across from a thickset man called Sonny, who seemed about ten years younger than me, with polished black hair, a strong handshake and wearing black trousers and a black knit polo shirt.

"Mandy said you had to see me," Sonny said, sitting down behind his cluttered desk.

"What's this about?"

I said, "My name's John Keegan. I'm retired Air Force, and for some years, I was stationed at McIntosh, back when it was active. Worked as a boom operator aboard the KC-135s, refueling aircraft. Ate a lot of your pizza, along with other people stationed here."

That produced a small smile. "Glad to hear it. Though when me and my brother opened the joint up, we didn't think we were going to make it at first. Only customers were you guys on the base... the rest of the towns around here weren't that built up yet."

I shifted in my seat. "Funny you should mention that, because that's why I stopped here today. To talk about the time when you first opened up."

"What do you mean?"

I stared right at him. "I mean, didn't you feel guilty at all, stealing all that cash from the military families living there, while their husbands and fathers were risking their lives to protect you and your country?"

***

Well, his face got as red as his pizza's tomato sauce, and he started yapping about tossing me out and beating me up and about a half-dozen other things, and when he caught his breath, I said, "You see, now that I'm retired, I have a lot of time on my hand. And one thing I do is run a website for Air Force veterans that were stationed here with me during the 1970s and 1980s. A good place to catch up on old friends, and swap stories and such. And one of the stories was about the number of break-ins and burglaries the base housing experienced during 1974. Back about the same time you and your brother opened this place. And that got me to thinking. With the spare time I've got, I got to thinking a lot."

"Bud," Sonny said, his voice low and mean, "you have sixty seconds to get out of my office, and out of my joint, without you getting your nose broken."

I went on. "Funny thing is, it was only the homes that got broken into that year. Never any place else. And the base security, they did the best they could, but they had more important things to do. Like keeping an eye on the aircraft and the hangars, ordinance, and everything else. Back then, I remembered some of the folks there thought it was bored kids living on base, just raising a bit of hell. But I didn't like that theory. It had to be somebody off base, somebody who had access... somebody who needed cash. Like you and your brother and your new restaurant."

Sonny was breathing so hard that his nostrils were flaring. I went on. "Made sense. Guy like you and your brother, making a pizza delivery inside to the families... and through gossip and such, you knew which homes might be empty. Just a quick break-in, grab some cash, and get out. What the heck, right? This was after the Vietnam war, so they're just Air Force trash. Too dumb to get better jobs in the real world. Was that what you were thinking?"

He said slowly, "You can't prove a goddamn thing."

I smiled. "Sonny, this is the Air Force we're talking about. Another big government agency that likes to keep track of things. I'm sure somewhere there are the visitor logs from that year, recording each time one of you guys went in to make a delivery. And it wouldn't take too much effort to cross-reference those delivery times with the records of the break-ins."

Now one hand was on his desk, fingers nervously tapping on some sheets of paper. "That's still not proof. And that happened a long, long time ago."

"Sure it did. But times have changed.

Technology's changed. And maybe back then you could get away with what you did to the military families on our air base. But people support the military today. It's not like it was back then, right after Vietnam. And technology... like I said, I run a little website. How do you think your business would survive if I posted pictures of your restaurant, with your phone number and address, and announced to the world how you stole from military families that year, terrorized them and frightened them, just so you and your brother could keep your pizza place running?"

If anything, his face seemed even more red, and I was waiting for another explosion when he surprised me. He took a deep breath and looked at me directly and said, "What do you want?"

"Not sure if I understand the question."

"Look, I'm not admitting anything. Not at all. But it's been a long, long time... so what do you want?"

From inside my coat I pulled out a business card, which I slid across the desktop to him. I said, "That's the highest-ranked military charity in the country, helping out families of wounded warriors... starting this week, Sonny, and for the foreseeable future, you're going to make a sizable donation to this charity, once a month. Say... a thousand dollars. And a friend of mine is on that charity's board of directors. So I'll know for certain whether you're making the donation or not."

He picked up the card, examined it like it was contaminated with anthrax or something. "Or what?"

"Or I'll go public."

"I can sue."

"Sure you can," I said. "And while your lawsuit works its way through the court system, just imagine the months of free, nasty publicity you're going to get, especially if other websites pick up the story, and pass it along, and pass it along."

Sonny looked at the card for a moment longer, and then dropped it on his desk. "All right... you've got a deal."

"Glad to hear it."

But he stared at me hard one more time and said, "You know, you're a real bastard."

I offered him a satisified smile. "Maybe so, but my birth certificate says otherwise. As for you, Sonny, being a bastard was a career choice."

Danger From Within

Janis Patterson

The dark rain slashed at the windows as if it held a personal grudge, making Ellen Patrick shiver even though she was warm and dry.

Wouldn't you know that this would happen after all the weeks of counting days and hours until she could fly to Tokyo! Now thanks to a gigantic typhoon she was stuck in a dreary airport USO instead of winging over the Pacific. It just wasn't fair. At least she was safe in here instead of stuck out in the main airport with hundreds of stranded and angry travelers.

"Here. You look like you need this."

Still self-consciously clumsy, Ellen reached up her left hand and took the extended coffee mug. The volunteer hostess made sure Ellen had it firmly before releasing the thick china. Her hand lettered name tag said Florene Hardy. Scarcely bigger than a child, the woman was wizened and white-haired and looked a thousand years old.

"How's your wrist?" she asked, nodding to the heavy bandage that seemed to swallow most of Ellen's right hand.

"It's okay. Hurts a little," she admitted, then in answer to Florene Hardy's unasked question, said, "Couple of cracked bones. I tripped over a box the day the movers came. You never seem to realize how much stuff you have until you have to move."

"That's the truth." Cradling her own well-used mug, Florene sat on the couch beside Ellen and looked out the window. "Real frog-strangler, that is. Wouldn't be surprised if they closed down the whole airport. Where's your husband stationed, Mrs. Patrick?" Florene had been careful to note Ellen's name when she signed in and showed her military ID card.

"Yokosuka, on Tokyo Bay. He's a Navy commander," Ellen added with undisguised pride. "It's been six months since I've seen him."

"Back during the War some wives didn't see their men for over four years. I was lucky. Only two years for me. My Jake came home shot up, but at least he came home."

There was no question as to what war she meant. "Things are better now," Ellen murmured.

"Not as long as there are wars," the old lady said in a hard voice. "Bad enough the young people get killed without some people making a profit."

Neither was there any question as to whom the old lady meant. He had come in not long after Ellen, griping against the weather and flight delays as if they were personal insults. Short and oblong like a shoebox, he wore an obviously expensive business suit, but it didn't make any difference how much it had cost; on him it looked like baggy sacking.

What had put Ellen's back up was that across the left side of his chest was a positive drapery of medals—on a business suit! Usually when someone had that many, they used just the ribbons to make neat bars of what was jokingly called fruit salad. These were the miniature medals, of course; not even Schwarzenegger would have enough chest space for that many full sized ones. Ellen couldn't help wondering if they were all legitimate.

"There's a lot of money to be made in security," he was saying in a booming voice big enough to fill an auditorium instead of just a good-sized room. "You can work five years and, if you're sensible, have enough money for the rest of your life. If I didn't have to leave in just a few minutes I could tell you about...."

His audience, two strapping young men and a strikingly pretty young woman with a hard face, all in utility cammies, appeared to be hanging raptly on every word.

The elderly volunteer snorted. "Security, my Aunt Fanny! Mercenaries is more like it. Wouldn't be surprised if he went from USO to USO recruiting."

"I'm surprised you let him in here," Ellen murmured.

"Had to. Colonel Arlen's an honorably discharged retiree."

"Colonel Arlen!" Ellen sat forward in surprise, almost choking on her coffee. "The Colonel Arlen who runs DB Worldwide Security?"

"The same." The old lady spit out the words as if they were rotten.

"But...." Ellen began, then her words faded in case the slightest breath of them should reach the pompous, notorious little man's ears. Some of Ryan's own men had followed the siren song of Colonel Arlen's 'security' company, and some of them had died in what were almost certainly dodgy situations. Ryan swore—privately, of course—that Arlen instigated wars and created conflict simply to create work—and profit—for DB Worldwide Security. Ryan also said that DB stood for Dirty Bastards, and Ellen had heard nothing to disprove it.

The lights flickered, then went out, silence rushing in as the computers and refrigerator ceased. Ellen shivered atavistically in spite of herself. For two long moments time was suspended, then with much blinking of lights and snarling of motors, the power came back on and stayed.

"First time that's happened in a long time," Florene muttered. "Nothing'll be getting out of here tonight. Too dangerous outside."

"Security is an honorable profession," Colonel Arlen blustered on. Ellen wondered if he had even noticed the power failure. "We can do so much more to help people and protect property as we are unhampered by tradition and outmoded custom...."

It sounded as if diminutive Florene were growling. Ellen wasn't feeling very charitable either; maybe she should say something...? After all, wasn't a big part of being an officer's wife keeping things running smoothly? She was saved from her sometimes unreliable tongue by the ringing of the telephone.

Florene jumped to answer it with an alacrity suited to someone half her years. "USO, Florene speaking." She nodded vigorously as she listened, as if the party at the other end of the line could see her, then after a lengthy time said, "I understand. Don't worry. I'll take care of things. No problem."

She hung up slowly, then turned towards the room, her face an unreadable study of strong emotions.

"We take good care of our people," Colonel Adair was saying. "Nothing but the best..."

"Listen to me, all of you!" the old woman said loudly in a voice that cracked oddly. "That was Homeland Security. They're afraid that a terrorist group is going to do an attack on the airport tonight, what with all the flights cancelled and the place full of people."

The three uniformed soldiers stood as one. "We'd better get out there, there," the older man —a corporal named Willoughby who looked all of twenty-five or so—said. "We can help with crowd control if nothing else."

"No!" Florene snapped. "I'm not supposed to let anyone leave." To illustrate her point she turned the key on the double-deadbolt, then removed the key and put it in her pocket before moving to the windows and closing the blinds one by one. "I'm to keep the door locked and the windows shuttered until the all clear, unless a legitimate visitor comes."

"But..."

"Perhaps the sight of your uniforms could precipitate something," Ellen said vaguely. "Perhaps they're trying to avoid that. Or maybe they're saving you three for a backup force."

"Doesn't make any sense," young Willoughby grumbled, but the three sat back down.

"Now that's the spirit we at DB Worldwide Security need!" Colonel Adair was effusive. "Courage. Ability to diagnose a potential problem. A...."

"Oh, shut up, you stupid old bag of shit," the young woman in Army cammies snapped, and the colonel recoiled as if she had struck him. Her anger made her even more beautiful. Now Ellen could see that her name tape said Obregon and her rank device proclaimed her to be a master sergeant.

"My dear young woman..."

"You wouldn't know courage if it bit you on the ass. You barely escaped court martial, and I think you should have been for your sorry-assed performance at Al-Kattab. Remember Al-Kattab? A lot of good men died that day simply because you were too stupid to know what needed to be done. Anyone who goes to work for you is a fool!" She stood jerkily and walked to furthest couch, anger radiating from her in palpable waves.

"Who did you lose?" Florene asked. Her tone was tender, but rusty, as if she hadn't used that emotion much in a long time.

"My brother. He was going career, and he'd have made it, too. He..." She bit the words off with a snap and flung herself down. Grabbing a magazine at random, she opened it and stared without seeing, isolating herself as unquestionably as if she had gone into a different room and slammed the door behind her.

"I assure you, young woman..."

"Can it!" snapped Corporal Willoughby. "You and your company are bad news."

"But the money..." said the other soldier, a private named Matabe who didn't look as if he were old enough to shave by himself, let alone enlist. "They pay..."

"Yeah. If you live long enough to get it.

Some of the guys from my unit joined up with him after they got out. Two got killed and the third got burned so bad he wished he had. This guy's only interested in the money he makes. Come on." Not giving the younger man a chance to disagree, Willoughby pulled him over to the far edge of the room.

The colonel's face had gone from its customary ruddiness to a pasty white and was now a mottled purple. His voice, however, was still mellifluous. "Well, it is a truism that when you have heroism, you sometimes have tragedy. It is also a truism that courage is shown by actions, not by words. Now, if we're going to be isolated for the rest of the night, I must make the best of it. Make me a sandwich, will you?" he asked—no, ordered—Florene without even giving her the courtesy of a look.

Ellen would have protested at that, but Florene shook her head and walked back behind the counter. After a moment Ellen followed, past the messy desk and into the tiny, overcrowded room behind that combined the functions of kitchenette and storeroom.

"You shouldn't have to put up with that, Mrs. Hardy. Isn't there something…?"

Her mouth a tightly puckered slit, Florene

looked up from a messy stack of white bread and lunch meat. At first she didn't seem inclined to answer Ellen; she dug in a cluttered drawer, withdrew a wicked-looking French chef's knife at least a foot long from the clattering mess and slashed the inoffensive sandwich as if it had been enemy flesh.

"He may be a bag of shit like that girl said, but he's an honorably retired veteran and he has the right to the full use of the USO facilities whether we like him or not."

Ellen had been considering asking for a sandwich for herself, but changed her mind as, the sandwich cut, Florene swabbed at the blade with a limp-looking dish-towel, then dumped the knife back into the bulging drawer. Between the casual cleaning and the chunk of handle missing right by the blade, the knife would be a prime breeding ground for all kinds of germs.

"And this area is reserved for volunteers only," Florene continued in the same hard monotone. "You'll have to go back to the public area."

Ellen did, sitting primly on the couch, an unread magazine open on her lap as Florene took the paper plate with the sandwich to Colonel Adair. He didn't, Ellen noticed, say thank you. Perhaps it would be a good thing if he did get food poisoning from that knife. It would serve him right, the pompous old windbag.

If she had thought to enjoy the sight of the colonel's discomfiture it wasn't going to happen, for within minutes the lights went out and, after a few hopeful flickers, stayed out. Predictably, the colonel raged against inefficiency, but no one paid him much attention.

Florene produced a tiny but powerful flashlight and calmly handed out pillows and comforters from the cache in the luggage storeroom. There was just enough light for Ellen to see that her comforter was spangled with grotesque superheroes ugly enough to populate nightmares. It didn't make any difference; the comforter was warm and with the power off the heat would go. Outside the rain seemed to have increased, howling with an almost human voice.

"Good night, everyone," Florene said. "Sleep well." It was a wasted admonition; two of the soldiers were already snoring enthusiastically.

Ellen knew it was good advice, but she couldn't follow it. Her wrist was throbbing just enough to keep her alert. She could have taken a pain pill—her doctor had given her a liberal supply—but as they always knocked her out for extended periods of time she didn't want to take them while still on the ground in fear she might miss something important. She had planned to take one right after the plane lifted off and sleep during the long trans-Pacific flight, but who knew when that would be now?

Instead she lay listening to the others snore and thinking of how wonderful it would be to be with Ryan again, making a home with him again. Once someone almost cried out, as in the throes of a dream, but it cut off and was not repeated. Twice someone got up to go to the bathroom, the rushing flush sounding almost like a flood inside the building. Once someone rummaged in the refrigerator, an action made clumsy in trying to be quiet and was followed by the crack and whoosh of a soft drink can being opened. Outside almost imperceptibly the rain slowed, finally dying to a thin pattering and finally Ellen dozed.

At approximately four-thirty the power blinked a time or two, then leapt to full life. Lights flooded the area with stabbing brilliance while heater, computers, refrigerator and Heaven only knew what else filled the air with a cacophony of background noise. They were all back into the twenty-first century and everything was as it was before.

Except it wasn't. Colonel Adair lay unmoving in his big recliner, the handle of a large knife protruding from his chest.

Ellen felt like screaming. She hadn't liked the man or what he did, but he was dead. A dead body in the same room with her! A man murdered in the same room with her and, what was worse, murdered by someone who was in this room right now. She had looked; the door was still locked.

Master Sergeant Obregon threw a comforter over the body, but it didn't really help. Somehow the great puffy lump spattered with printed roses seemed just as obscene as what it covered.

"How did the terrorists get in?" Matabe asked; his voice seemed to have risen at least an octave. "Do you think he was their target?"

"No one came in," Ellen said. "The door is still locked."

"And that means one of us did it." Obregon's voice was hard.

Florene gave a great shuddering sigh and crumpled in on herself, looking as if she were made of tissue paper and would disintegrate at a touch. Willoughby and Obregon caught her just as she sagged and put her on the couch where Ellen had slept.

Pale light from outside leaked in the windows and there was a sullen roar from a jet engine somewhere. Willoughby opened the blinds. The sky was still dark, but the great vapor lights were on, illuminating the vast concrete expanses with an ugly orange glow.

"Looks normal out there," he said. "I guess everything is over."

Master Sergeant Obregon could not take her eyes from the masking comforter. "Not in here."

It was Ellen who called airport security. The desk phone worked, somewhat to Ellen's surprise; no one had had a cell phone, except maybe the colonel, but no one wanted to touch the body. Ellen had to go into Florene's pocket to get the door key, as the old woman seemed incapable even of that.

At first glance the airport policeman looked just like any other policeman at the end of a tiring shift; a rumpled uniform, a hang-dog face.

"Is the emergency over?" Ellen asked. "Did you get the terrorists?"

He studied each of them with a penetrating

look that went clear to the bone, then lifted the comforter just enough to see.

"What terrorists? That who I think it is?"

"Yes, it's Colonel Arlen of DB Worldwide Security. What do you mean, what terrorists?" Ellen was brusque, a predictable reaction to the tension building inside her. "Wasn't the airport under lockdown last night because of a terrorist threat? Florene was told to lock the door and not let anyone in or out."

Officer Raggio, according to his nametag, looked at Ellen as if she were feebleminded. "There was a storm last night, a real typhoon that knocked out the power and shut down the airport for a couple of hours. There wasn't anything said about terrorists."

"So who made the call?" Ellen asked.

Obviously dismissing her, Raggio's gaze flicked to Master Sergeant Obregon. "What happened in here?"

The Army did indeed make strong men, even if it was a woman. Obregon gave an unvarnished account of the evening, including her outburst at the colonel. After the lights went out, she said, she had gone to sleep and hadn't waked until the lights came on.

Willoughby and Matabe each gave

approximately the same story. Willoughby said he had gone to the bathroom, while Matabe confessed that he had not only gone to the bathroom, he had raided the refrigerator.

"I was so thirsty," he said, body ramrod straight but eyes firmly focused on the floor. "You couldn't see a thing, and I tried to be quiet, but the cans rattled. All I wanted was a Coke. I got," he said, a flash of distaste distorting his features, "some kind of fruity something. The can's over there under the table."

"What did you do to your wrist?" Raggio asked Ellen suddenly, startling her.

"I tripped over a box the day the movers came. I'm going to Japan to join my husband. We'll be there two years."

"You willing to let a doctor look at that?"

"My doctor has already... Oh. You mean you want to know if I'm really injured." Ellen's stomach tightened and flip-flopped. He actually thought she might have murdered the colonel! "Of course I will."

"Way I see it," Raggio said with ponderous gravity, "any one of you could have done it, except Miz Hardy here, and, if Miz Patrick's injury is real, her. Takes strength to stab a man, and don't think either of them could have done it. You three, though—any of you could."

Ellen was torn between elation at exoneration and pique that this... this *flatfoot!*... should think so little of her. She knew, however, that she was innocent and at this moment it didn't look like Florene could cut a sandwich, let alone stab a man. On the other hand, it was hard to believe that any three such nice young soldiers could be guilty.

But there wasn't anyone else. It had to be someone here, someone who had slept in this room with her last night.

"Now you all sit down and be quiet," Raggio ordered. "I'm going to call in the detectives. And don't none of you touch nothing." He wandered off to the area by the door, muttering into his radio.

Obregon sat in a straight chair, her face ghostly pale. "I'll admit I wanted the bastard dead," she said, "but I didn't do it."

"Me, neither," said Willoughby.

"I didn't do it," Matabe squeaked. His eyes were all but standing out of his head.

"There's no one else," Ellen murmured. "We were the only ones in here last night, the door was locked, and I can't see the colonel committing suicide."

"So who was it?" Willoughby asked, looking at each of them in turn. "Who killed Colonel Arlen?"

Ellen had always been cursed with a logical mind, and now it was working overtime, bringing forth questions and conclusions she really didn't want to consider. Ignoring Raggio's outraged roar, she lifted the comforter, exposing the knife handle. The chipped and cracked knife handle. It was all the proof she needed.

"Why," she asked in soft and sorrowful tones, "did you kill him, Florene?"

The old woman lifted her head so slowly they could almost hear the muscles and bones creaking like rusted machinery. For a moment it seemed as if she wouldn't answer, then at last she sighed. "Because he needed killing, that's why. Before he could get any more young people killed. How did you know?"

"Lots of things. There was no terrorist threat, but you were the one who said there was. Who called?"

"Janie Grayson. Said she couldn't come in to do her shift. Seemed like a gift, my being here with Arlen. I had to stop him from leaving, so I said there was a security lock-down."

"And the rest?" Obregon asked. "How did

you know, Mrs. Patrick?"

"The knife. I saw Florene cutting the colonel's sandwich with it. She put it away just before the lights went out."

"So anyone could have gotten it," Raggio scowled, but Ellen shook her head.

"The drawer is back in that crowded kitchen area and full of all kinds of things. No one who didn't know this place very well could have found or removed it without making a lot of noise. I was awake all night, and the only noise was Private Matabe rummaging in the refrigerator."

In spite of himself Raggio was interested. "That old lady couldn't stab a man like the colonel. She's too weak."

"Arlen was sleeping," Ellen said, the memory of an abortive cry surfacing. "And strong emotion makes us strong."

"Who of yours did he get killed, Mrs. Hardy?" Obregon asked gently. She knelt by the fragile old lady and took her hand.

"My grandson. At Al-Kattab." Florene drew a shuddering breath as if living itself had become a burden, then looked at Ellen. "I'm not sorry. If ever a man deserved killing, he did. I had to take my chance while I had it."

"People have been trying to kill that bastard for years," Willoughby muttered, "and no one could ever do it. I guess he felt safe in here."

At least Ryan wouldn't be the only one happy that Colonel Adair could no longer put young people at foolish risk, Ellen thought. Aloud she said, "He never realized that the greatest danger always comes from within."

An Officer and a Gentleman's Agreement

Barb Goffman

West Point, New York. 1972.

"Holy mother of God! What have you done?"

I finished off the exclamation point at the end of "Beat Navy!," which I'd just spray painted on the grass near where the bonfire would soon be lit. Next to the goat. It was warm for early December, but I could still see my breath in the moonlight as I turned and smiled at my roommate, Pete.

"Pretty cool, huh?" We were going to go down in cadet history as having pulled off the best prank ever!

Pete's mouth hung open as he tried to form some words. What was his problem?

"How could you have done this?" Pete finally said. "You killed him. You killed Bill the Goat!"

I glanced down at the Navy mascot. His

white coat, the grass beneath him, and the big N on the jacket the squids made him wear were stained red. The metallic smell of blood invaded my nose.

An hour ago I'd driven to the abandoned barn where Pete and I'd stashed the goat, alive, early this morning after driving all night back from Maryland. I painted its horns Army black and gold then wrestled him again into the back of Pete's station wagon to bring him to campus. It had been no small task sneaking him past the sentry. Killing him at the barn would have been a lot easier, but I hadn't wanted to get blood all over Pete's car.

"So? What are you so upset about?" I slipped the paint can into my coat pocket, pulled out Pete's car keys, and tossed them to him. "It's just a stupid animal. Besides it crapped all over the back of your car last night. You should be thrilled."

Pete stared at me. "Thrilled? What the hell is wrong with you, Jack? The plan was to bring Bill back here, paint his horns, show him off, get a little glory before tomorrow's Army-Navy game, and then return him! Alive!"

"Don't get your panties in a twist. It's not like old Bill here hasn't been goat-napped before.

Where's the glory in that? Now this"—I pointed a thumb at the carcass—"this will bring us fame beyond your imagination."

"Fame? More like infamy." Pete paced back and forth for a few moments, shaking his head. "It's one thing to kill an animal for food, but to slit its throat for... for what? Fun? You think this is fun?"

"Yeah, I do. I never realized you were such a wuss, Pete."

I surveyed my work. "Beat Navy!" in big gold letters. Right underneath: the stinking Navy goat. This was the coolest thing any cadet at West Point had ever done. How could Pete not get that?

I heard voices approaching and grabbed Pete's arm. "Come on." I yanked him behind some big bushes. "You can see for yourself how great everyone else is gonna think this is."

A couple of cadets came from the direction of the mess hall. Probably plebes. I didn't recognize them.

"Holy crap!" the one with the orange hair said as they spotted the goat and rushed over. "It's the Navy mascot."

I nudged Pete and mouthed the word, "See?"

"I'm going to be sick," the other plebe said as they bent over the goat. "Is this someone's idea of a joke?"

"No one I know," Carrot Top said. "You'd have to pretty warped to murder a goat."

"We better tell someone," the other plebe said. "I hope they catch whoever did this and shoot him. Psychotic bastard."

"Shoot him and then expel him," Carrot Top said as they ran off.

I swallowed hard. Psychotic? Warped? How did they not get how great this was? A prank worthy of the best college in the country. In the world. I should be adored for this, not reviled.

Pete stood and started walking away, his hands stuffed in his pockets.

"Hey, where are you going?"

He turned to me, his eyes hard and cold. "I'm going to the commandant. I'm going to tell him how we kidnapped Bill. I'm going to tell him everything."

I sprang up and blocked his way. "Oh no, you're not. Go cry in your girlie journal if you want, but keep your mouth shut. You're not going to let your guilty conscience ruin my life."

"You may not care about the honor code,

Jack, but I do. Out of my way."

"No. Look, I thought this would be funny. A joke. How was I to know that no one would get it?" He tried to push past me. "You can't say anything, Pete. You can't do that to me."

"It's all about you, huh, Jack?"

I saw my future slipping away and thought fast. "No, it's about you, too. You spill your guts, and I'll do the same. I'll tell them how it was all your idea to go to Maryland. How we took your car. How you goaded me into it. Held the goat down while you had me do your dirty work."

"You lying son of a—"

"They'll believe me, Pete, once they see how distraught I am. Just you watch. Besides, I'm near the top of our class. I'll get away with a slap on the wrist, and in the spring, I'll get my commission. But you, old buddy, you'll be silenced and expelled. Your life destroyed. How do you think your pop the colonel will feel about that?"

I held my breath. Would he buy it?

His face paled as the wind coming off the Hudson River picked up. He bought it. Now to close the deal.

"Look, neither of us has to pay for this... mistake," I said. "You go clean out the wagon. I'll wash my hands and pitch my shirt and the spray paint where no one will find them. And we'll both keep our mouths shut. No one ever has to know."

"I'll know." Pete chewed on his lower lip so long, I thought I'd lost him. But then he nodded his agreement. "Don't ever speak to me again," he said as he turned away. "Our friendship is over."

I rolled my eyes. Like that was a big loss.

***

Great Falls, Virginia. 2010.

As I stepped into the kitchen from the garage, the mingled scents of lemon and garlic made my stomach grumble. I scanned the Tuscan-style furnishings. No pots on the stove. No plates on the table. I know I smelled food. Where the heck was Sandra? And more important, where was dinner?

The sound of the glass door off the deck sliding open answered my first question.

"Jack, there you are," Sandra said, coming inside.

She looked just right in that yellow dress I like—the one that made other men eat their hearts out. Their wives might be old and dried up, but just the sight of Sandra still excited me.

You'd never know she just turned fifty.

"I was afraid you forgot about dinner," she said.

"Dinner?"

She gave me her exasperated look, eyebrows shot to the sky, head tilted to the right. "Yes, dinner with my friend Deb and her husband. I reminded you this morning."

Christ. The book club friend. She'd been pleasant enough the couple times I'd met her, but to have to eat dinner with her *and* her husband? I just put in a long freaking day at the Pentagon, and now I had to spend the evening being polite and friendly.

Sandra pulled a glass bowl from the fridge. Looked like gazpacho. "C'mon. I've set out some bread and tapenade, and we have a nice bottle of Pinot open."

I suppressed a sigh and stepped outside, glad for the privacy the battalion of trees in our backyard provided, despite the leaves that sometimes dropped into the pool. At least I didn't always have to smile at annoying neighbors.

As Sandra began introductions, Deb—even pudgier than I remembered—stood. A scarecrow of a guy rose beside her. "Jack, you remember

Deb. I'd like you to meet her husband, Peter."

No way. *No freaking way.* His hair was gray and receding, and lines marred his face, but he otherwise hadn't changed much. I grinned and said hello to the wife, then stuck my hand out at Pete. "You old goat."

He smiled tightly—the kind of expression subordinates have after I've chewed them out and they have to take it. "Jack." He shook my hand fast and hard. "It's been a long time."

"You two know each other?" Sandra said. "That's wonderful. From where?"

"Back at the Academy." I settled into my favorite deck chair as Sandra handed me a goblet of wine. A hint of citrus wafted from it. "Pete and I were in the same class."

"What a small world," Sandra said as she eased into her usual chair. "Deb, did you know about these two?"

Deb shook her head, eyeing her husband. "No. Peter didn't mention it when he suggested this dinner. But then he never talks about those days. In fact, he doesn't like to talk about his time in the Army at all."

"Yeah, I heard you washed out after Nam," I said. "How'd your old man feel about that?"

Sandra shot me a look, but I wanted to see

how far I could push Pete.

His fists clenched. "I read about your nomination in the *Post* last week, Jack." Pete's voice was steady, but I'd scored a direct hit. "Chairman of the Joint Chiefs of Staff. Quite an accomplishment."

I let a big smile cross my face. "It's nice when the president appreciates your work."

"I bet it is." Pete downed some of his wine. "Whoever would've thought you'd get so far in your career?"

"Jack's going to be a four-star general." Sandra beamed.

Deb offered congratulations while Pete chewed his lower lip. He was jealous! I nearly laughed.

"Big job," Pete said. "You'll be chief military adviser to the president?"

You bet your ass I will. "That's right."

"The Senate has to approve your nomination?" Pete asked.

"Yep."

For a split second, I could've swore I saw a gleam in Pete's eyes.

"Hmm," he said. "Hope that goes okay."

***

The following Tuesday at fifteen hundred

hours I stepped into the darkness of the Old Brogue Irish Pub, a few miles from my house. The place reeked of fried food. Pete had suggested it yesterday on the phone. Said it shouldn't be crowded. We could talk. I wasn't sure what he wanted to talk about, but I figured I'd hear him out.

I ordered a Guinness at the bar and spotted Pete. He wasn't hard to find. There were only three people in there, besides the bartender. Pete had parked himself with his back to the wall at a table in the far corner. The other two patrons sat at the bar—two old guys arguing about the Washington Nationals as the game blared on an overhead TV.

I set my beer on Pete's sticky table and sat. "Charming place."

"It'll do." He leaned forward. "I've spent most of the past week thinking about you, Jack. You said you heard I ... how'd you so delicately phrase it? Oh yeah, 'washed out after Nam.'"

I smirked.

"Well, you should know that I've kept some tabs on you, too," Pete said. "I may not have stayed in the Army, but I have plenty of friends who did. And I've heard the rumors."

"Rumors?"

"The whispers about you. About the chances you've taken. The lives you've risked. And lost."

"Aah." I waved my hand at him. If he were a gnat, I'd have swatted him away. "Is this what you wanted to talk about? Lies made up by jealous personnel?"

"I heard about Desert Storm. You got promoted on the backs of innocent civilians. Dead civilians. Women. Children."

My face began feeling hot. Who was this turd to talk about me?

"And then Afghanistan. You managed to deflect blame in that friendly fire incident, but folks still know what you did."

"You don't know what you're talking about." It took all my strength to keep my voice low, when I really wanted to push the table aside and punch his face in.

"I know you're the same guy you were at the Academy. I could tell that from one evening at your house. You make excuses. You'll do anything for glory. You don't care who you hurt or who you have to scare or threaten to keep your secrets."

"You better watch yourself, Pete."

He lifted a manila folder off the wooden

chair beside him, opened it up, and scattered a slew of papers on the table. Copies of newspaper articles about that damn goat. Some from 1972, but others from throughout that decade, and the '80s, the '90s. Even one dated last year. Jesus.

"You're dragging out this old tale," I said. "Who cares? You think you can scare me with this?"

He stubbed his finger at the most-recent article. "They've never given up trying to figure out who killed Billy. It's been a black eye on the Academy all these years. And it's been the memory that's rotted my gut. I didn't wash out after Nam. I left. I couldn't bear to lead a platoon anymore, not when I didn't truly have honor. You stole that from me, Jack."

"Stole it?" I laughed. "Either you have honor, Pete, or you don't. Don't blame your failings on me."

He sipped his beer, sat quietly for a moment. "You're right," he said. "My biggest mistake was letting you use my father against me. My fear of disappointing him. So I kept my mouth shut, broke the code, and lost my honor. And that's on me."

What a pansy.

He leaned in again. "But you murdered the

Navy mascot. And that, Jack, is on you. You think the Senate will confirm your nomination if they learn what you did? Not in this day and age, old pal."

"Dream on. You have no proof."

He laughed. "I don't need proof. The allegations would be enough to do you in. So do yourself a favor. Withdraw your nomination and retire. Save your wife the embarrassment of learning who you really are." He stood and threw down a ten-dollar bill. It landed on top of the articles. "You can keep those. I have my own copies. You've got forty-eight hours, Jack. Do the right thing, or I'll spill my guts."

Pete brushed past me. I leapt up, grabbed his arm, and bent toward his ear. "You talk about honor. Well, we had an agreement all those years ago to keep our little prank between ourselves. You want to have honor? Honor that."

He shook my hand away. "That's the difference between us, Jack. You still think it was a harmless prank. I let you build your career on that dead goat. I let a man capable of that atrocity go on to rise through the ranks of our military. There's no honor in that."

Seething, I watched him walk away. When he neared the door, I followed him out. Watched him get in his silver Lexus. Memorized his license plate.

Who had forty-eight hours, Pete?

* * *

Four weeks later, I strode through a Senate hallway in my full dress uniform, my rack of fruit salad prominent on my chest. I'd earned every one of those medals and ribbons, and I wanted the whole world to see them.

The Committee on Armed Services had begun its hearing on my nomination early this morning, and things were proceeding just fine. As they should. No tough questions. No scandal like Pete had threatened. The senators had treated me with the respect I deserved. My future—and legacy—were secured.

It was too bad about Pete. But he'd brought it on himself. That terrible accident.

The post-lunch hallway was crowded. I shook a few hands and slapped some backs as I approached the hearing room. The afternoon session would begin in a couple minutes. I headed toward my seat.

As I strode up the aisle, I slowed. Who was that sitting at the other witness table? It looked like... No, it couldn't be.

I walked closer. *Deb?*

I hadn't seen her since the funeral. Sandra

said she hadn't been doing well. That she'd been holed up in her house, going through Pete's things. Practically clinging to them. What was she doing here? Now?

She reached out for the pitcher of water on the table. I spotted a manila folder open in front of her. Jesus, those damn goat articles! My heart sped up. That dumb bitch was going to try to ruin me.

I forced myself to take some deep breaths. I'd faced tougher adversaries before. I'd just discredit her. She didn't know anything. She had no proof.

"If you'll all take your seats," the committee chairman announced, "we're about to reconvene."

I glared at Deb while I pulled back my chair, and I noticed a few books laid out before her. Books with blank gold covers. They looked so familiar, but from where?

The chairman called the hearing to order, and as I settled into my seat, my memory clicked: Pete's girlie journals from West Point. The ones I'd made fun of. The ones he'd written in every day about his dreams and his failures.

And all his secrets.

Warriors Know Their Duty

S. M. Harding

Joe watched the guy walk down the street, trying to figure out what was off. Navy top coat whipped open by the spring wind, blue pinstripe suit, blue and red silk tie. Brown loafers.

"It's the shoes," Joe said. "Nobody would wear brown with that suit."

Benny shifted his gaze from the tall blond. "Clothes don't fit, neither. Suit's two sizes too large."

"He's nervous. Maybe downsized, going to a job interview."

"Bet he don't hear 'overqualified.' Not with the way he's holding his shoulders, all tense and defensive." Benny laughed. "I don't got that problem, never will."

Joe shifted on the park bench, rubbed his knee. "Something squirrely about that guy."

"You been looking for spooks for forty years," Benny said as he fingered his scraggly beard. "This ain't Saigon and that's just a nervous guy in a bad suit."

"Quin Nhon, and I was the spook for thirty years." He crossed his arms, motioned with his chin. "Look at the haircut. It's just plain wrong."

Benny pushed himself off the bench, tucked the newspaper under his arm. "Let it go, Joe. I'm gonna get coffee. You coming?"

"Nice day to sit and watch the world go by." He crossed his legs, moved an arm to the back of the bench. "Why's he carrying a Haliburton case?"

"Aw, Jesus. See you tomorrow."

Joe watched him walk away, then returned his attention to the bank building across Meridian Street.

***

"You seen the paper?" Benny asked the next morning as he settled on the bench. "Bank robbery right across the street yesterday and here we sat like bimbos at the bar waiting for Prince Charming."

"Be careful who you call a bimbo." Joe uncrossed his arms, stuck his beefy hand out. "Let me see the paper."

Benny handed it over, watched as Joe read the front page story.

"Pretty much what I figured," he said,

handing it back.

"Oh come on. Give me a break, Joe. How the hell did you know anything, sitting on a park bench?"

"I was here. You were having coffee." He pointed to the bank. "One squirrel goes into the bank looking nervous. Twenty minutes later, he comes out looking smug. Then he ducks into Mickey D's, goes into the john. When he comes out, he's dressed in casual clothes and has a backpack."

"How could you know it was the same guy?"

Joe gave him The Look, a unique combination of disdain, disgust, and pity.

"OK, OK, Eagle Eye recognized the perp from this distance."

"The haircut was a wig that didn't fit so good."

"Hmpf. So did you follow him?"

"I waited for the Haliburton case."

"Why don't you just tell me what the hell happened?" Benny threw the paper in the trash barrel while he tried The Look.

"I thought you'd like to exercise your gray matter for a change. Evidently, you don't have any left."

"Probably never had none," Benny said. "I was just a grunt in Nam with rotting feet and no officer's club, not some Special Forces honcho."

Joe crossed his arms, looked at the lowering sky. "I kept my eye on the door—good thing it's an old storefront, because there's only one door. Strolled across the street, took a post where I could cover the door. A guy comes out with a canvas suitcase."

"One of those new ones with rollers? If I ever traveled anymore, I'd get me one of those."

"No rollers. Big enough to hold the Haliburton though. He walks over to the bus stop, so I follow. Number 18 comes, he gets on, I get on. Find a seat behind him."

"Jesus, did you call the cops?"

"Of course not. I was going on gut feeling and experience. I figured these two guys were working together, plus the team who was holding the bank manager's family—no, at that point I didn't know about that part, but there weren't any alarms going off, no cop cars rushing the bank. So he must've done something to keep things quiet until he was long gone. I figured the first guy and the guy I was tailing would meet up to split up the take."

"How the hell did you know there was a

bank robbery going down in the first place?"

Joe shrugged. "How could I not?"

"Oh, brother."

"So I was on the bus, the guy with the canvas suitcase was way up in front and I was in the middle. We were up by the Children's Museum and damn if he didn't jump off just as the doors were closing. I got off the next stop, but by the time I walked back with this bum leg, he was gone."

"Aw Jesus." Benny leaned back on the bench. "So what'd the cops say?"

"I didn't talk to them. Look, Benny, this was para-military ops, I'm sure of it. Four man team, half at the manager's house, half to pull the switch in Mickey D's. Probably one of these militia groups trying to take over the government. Half-mil would buy big armaments. Ground-to-air missile, maybe a dirty bomb. We're in for a rough time until we find the bastards."

"How the hell do you get from a weird-looking guy to blowing up Indianapolis?"

"Easy, my friend, if you have the experience."

"Aw, you're just looking for some excitement. Ain't anybody gonna blow up Indy."

"President's coming in on Friday. These militias would do anything to take him down, especially with his latest Supreme Court nominee."

"You're kidding. You gotta be kidding. A presidential assassination here? By a bunch of guys who play paint ball on the weekends? Sheeze."

"Go ahead, keep your head in the sand. Look at what that cell in Michigan was planning. Kill police officers to start the uprising. They're not playing paint ball, they're playing hardball, Benny."

"Why didn't you talk to the cops?"

"I'd get all entangled in Homeland Security and a dozen federal agencies and couldn't do a damn thing to stop this plot."

"Do? By yourself? Oh, Mother of Mercy."

"Well, Benny," Joe said, leaning toward Benny and putting an arm around his shoulders. He opened his cell phone and showed the picture to him. "I've got a plan."

***

Benny was sweating like a glass of iced tea on the hottest day of summer. He'd kept asking Joe why Joe couldn't do this himself and Joe kept saying he didn't have this kind of contact.

Local. Easiest route. No sweat.

OK, Benny knew a lot of cops, had grown up with a lot of them. His oldest friend was a homicide detective. So what? This was a damn bank job, nothing to do with murder. Unless Joe's scenario was right. He should know, all those years with Special Forces and the CIA. But he should be here to meet with Lou. Benny felt useless to get what Joe wanted without spilling the beans.

The smell of stale cigarette smoke still hung in the bar though it'd been a year since anyone had smoked in the place. Benny could do with a cigarette, even though he hadn't smoked in twenty-five years. Instead, he shredded the cocktail napkin.

"Hey, Benny," Lou said, sliding into the booth. "You look like you lost your best friend."

"You're here, so it must not be true." Benny signaled to the bartender. "I got a favor to ask, so I'm buying."

"A favor? What, you need a ticket fixed? I don't do that shit, Benny."

"Nothing like that. It's complicated and I can only tell you part of it."

The bartender put a Bud down in front of Lou and another Pepsi on the table by Benny.

"What I need is for you to run a photo through that new facial recognition program you been jawing about."

"Who of?"

"Well if I knew that, I wouldn't be asking you to run it. Of a, er..., a suspect."

"Suspect for what? And why aren't you going to the district station?"

"I told you, it's complicated." He finished off his drink, pulled the new one close. "I just need you to run it, nothing official."

"Benny, what's going on?"

"Can't you just do that? Take it on faith I ain't doing nothing illegal?"

"Asking me to do this without cause is illegal." He examined the glass, poured the beer with a good head. "It's not that I don't trust you, you know I do. But I need to know more."

"It's a need-to-know thing," Benny said, regretting the words as soon as he'd said them. He looked up. "Just kidding."

Lou just stared at him.

"It's about the bank job, but I ain't saying nothing else."

"The big heist downtown?"

Benny nodded, miserable. Afraid he'd already said too much.

"Did you witness it?"

"Wasn't in the bank."

"Where were you?"

"Look, all I need is for you to run the damn photo." He slid a manilla envelope across the table. "Is that asking too much for a guy who pulled you out of the way of a sniper and took the bullet?"

Lou sat back, crossed his arms. "You've never played that card. This must be important."

"It is. Wouldn't you get credit if you cracked the case?"

"Benny, I'm a year away from retirement. I don't need another commendation."

"Couldn't hurt, maybe get you a reward."

"Why don't you just tell me what this is about?"

"Can't. Honest. I promised."

"Who?"

Benny shook his head.

Lou leaned slightly forward. "The benchmate you're always talking about? Joe Custer?"

Benny refused to meet his stare. "Yes or no, Lou. You could say I got mugged and can't make it down to the station. Or a hit and run. Whatever. You're a captain, nobody's going to question you. Nobody needs to know I'm an old army buddy."

They listened to the bar chatter, the game turned down low on the TV, the clink of glasses. Neither man moved.

"OK. One run through the program," Lou said, sliding out of the booth. He stood. "On one condition: you tell me what the hell's going on if we get a hit."

***

Joe slid nonchalantly onto the bench, didn't look at Benny. Instead, he looked at the overcast sky, heavy clouds promising rain soon. "So, did you get an ID?"

"Yeah."

"You don't sound excited about it," Joe said, glancing at Benny. "We can track these guys down, stake them out, take them down before they know what's happening. Man!"

"Don't think it's gonna happen that way."

"Why not? What's the address?"

"Unknown."

"Hell. Last known?"

"About ten years ago," Benny said, still not looking at Joe. "In Kansas City."

"Ah, a recruiter. Should've known. There's got to be some way to track them down here.

They'll be in town until the President's toast. And most of the city's just a shell."

Benny sat, watched two more undercover cops go into Mickey D's. "Don't think so." He worked his jaw.

"What's the matter with you? Are you going to chicken out?" Joe shook his head. "I don't believe it. The President of the United States is in jeopardy and you're not willing to work this?"

"Joe, you're full of shit." He turned to face him. "Your bank robber is just that. Got a rapsheet that goes back to the mid-90s. No militia. No plot to blow Indy to hell and back. One stupid ass bank robber. Working alone."

Joe turned to him. "How'd you work this out? Are you sure?"

"Positive. The money was still there in the damn Haliburton case in the false ceiling above the john with his prints all over it."

"You looked?"

Benny shook his head. "Lou did."

A thin man with a shock of white hair walked toward the bench, shook hands with Benny, and sat between the two men.

Benny leaned forward, looked at Joe. "I'd like you to meet Captain Lou Howard, homicide division, IMPD."

Lou put out his hand. Joe hesitated, then shook it.

"I'd like to thank you for your acute observational skill in identifying the perpetrator of the Fletcher National Bank office," Lou said. "However, next time I'd advise you to alert the police. And concoct less ambitious theories." He stood, grinned at Benny, and sauntered away.

"Ambitious theories, my ass. You guys got lucky this time, but next—"

"Won't be a next time. Not for me," Benny said, looking Joe in the eye. "You miserable sonofabutt. Your time in-country was all of a month, wasn't it? Not at a forward base because there weren't any by the time you got there. And a CIA agent? Black ops? Parachuting into Iran during the hostage crisis? All a bunch of horsefeathers. After the Army, you went to work for a security company and wracked up your leg falling off a damn ladder checking a damn security camera at a liquor store."

"Ah, Benny, I can explain – "

Benny got up, began to walk away.

"You really think local cops can check up on a CIA agent?" Joe yelled.

Benny kept walking.

Salome's Gift

Diana Catt

The package sat on the kitchen table begging to be opened and I could hardly restrain myself. It had just arrived by UPS, special delivery from Iraq, addressed to me. I knew it was my birthday present from my brother, Cain, but I also knew there'd be hell to pay if I delayed my chores to open it.

I was draining the dishwater, casting eager glances at the package, when I caught the faint hum of an engine. I listened closely. It was definitely on our road, but still about a half-mile down below from the sound of it. Not the UPS van returning; not Dad's pick-up, either, although he and Mom were due home anytime. It was rare to have two visitors to our mountain-top home in one week, let alone two in one day. The promise of an exciting birthday hung in the air.

Free from chores at last, I ignored the visitor's approach and turned to the package. I tore into the sealed box. Inside were two gifts, identically wrapped in bright orange paper. The tag on one read "To Salome". I was surprised to see the other tag read "To Marlena", Cain's girlfriend. Her birthday was next month.

I ran my finger across the satiny orange paper and admired the crisp corners and folds. The military precision made me miss my brother so much it hurt. I carefully lifted out the twin gifts and spotted an envelope addressed to me in Cain's familiar cursive, in the bottom of the box. I placed both presents on the table top, opened the envelope and read the letter.

My Dear Sali,

Today little Salome is 14. Happy 14th! Wish I could give you a big hug. I've watched you become a beautiful person. Hope you like the gift. Sorry, but no way to exchange it. I'm doing fine, but missing you and Mom and Marlena. Even missing Dad! Imagine that! Heard tell of a rumor that we could get sent home on leave soon. Like next month! Keep that a secret—don't want Mom to get depressed if the info is false. Enjoy your big day and blow out all the candles. Bet you're driving the boys crazy. Sending all my love to you.

Love,

Cain

PS -Be assured that your gift was something I bought especially for you, but then went back and got the second as an afterthought. Can you keep it hidden somewhere in your closet until Marlena's birthday next month? You're the best sister ever. Enjoy the gift.

I read it again. Then once more, slowly, trying to decipher Cain's hidden code; there always was one. When he was about ten and I only five, he started sending me secret messages. For years I thought everyone learned to read that way. Every letter he sends home has a special message for my eyes only. Today, however, I was too excited about the unopened present to get my decipher key.

I stared intently at the two orange gifts as if I had x-ray vision. I lifted them up to eye level. They seemed identical in size, shape and weight. But mine was special. He'd picked it out just for me.

In the background of my excitement, I heard the approaching vehicle's engine struggling and gears grinding. No local would attempt our road this time of year without four-wheel drive. Spring melt-off usually meant precarious wash-outs and mudslides. I figured I could probably see the top of the car on the switchback below if I looked out the bedroom window. But first, I took a moment to hide Marlena's gift. I secreted it in old purse in the back of my closet then reread Cain's letter, satisfied that Marlena's gift was hidden to his specs.

That's when I heard the engine sputter to a stop outside. The visitor had arrived.

I peeked out my bedroom window. No wonder it'd had problems climbing up our drive; it was a taxi. My heart sped up as a man in uniform stepped out of the back, then just as suddenly froze as a second uniformed man emerged and I realized neither was Cain. The memory of Cain's deep voice echoed in my mind, reassuring me not to worry about him unless we were visited by military personnel.

My mountain world froze. The birds went silent; the breeze stopped. Time itself was interrupted. This couldn't be happening. I collapsed to the floor in tears, hugging Cain's letter to my broken heart.

I didn't hear the knock at the door. I didn't know time was passing. I didn't hear Dad's truck arrive. I stirred a bit at Mom's cry of anguish but then sank deeper into myself; into a pit of darkness and despair. Dad found me in my room and lifted me into an embrace, his face a mask of stern lines.

It wasn't until Marlena arrived that I understood Cain was missing, not dead. There was hope, however horrible the situation, there was hope. Mom called friends and relatives, contacted the ladies in the prayer chain from church, and we received more worried visitors that evening than our mountain home had seen in a year. At bedtime, I slipped off to my room and tried to read my letter from Cain once more, but my heart was too heavy. I tucked it away into my night stand drawer. Marlena found me crying and held me until sleep overtook my fearful mind.

A week passed without any news. Our military liaison, Lt. Rita Parker, endlessly recounted cases where MIA were found weeks or months or even years later. Years. My God.

The unopened orange gift was an ominous

presence. I couldn't bear open it, but neither could I hide it away. Mom positioned it on the window sill of my room as if it were a candle beckoning the lost home

I began to hate Lt. Rita Parker and everything military. Cain would still be here if not for them. I had trouble dealing with the most mundane chores. Even making my bed was painful. The neatly folded corners that I previously strived to achieve only reminded me of Cain.

Marlena came over every day. On day nine of our nightmare, the taxi returned. Again, two uniformed men emerged from the back seat and they each carried a duffle bag. Marlena spotted the visitors through the window and let out a yelp of excitement. My injured heart gave a cautionary stir, but I couldn't move toward the door. I was paralyzed in place. Marlena, however, flew to the front door and threw it open wide, her expression expectant

"You're Marlena, Cain's girl," the dark-haired GI said. He was tall and lanky, with a soul patch decorating his chin.

Marlena nodded. "I have a picture of you," she said. "With him."

I was miraculously released from my

paralysis and moved to the doorway. I took Marlena's hand.

"And you're Salome," the blond man said. "We're friends of Cain."

Marlena took a step backward, opening the way into our home, inviting them in.

"Do you know where he is?" I asked. "Do you have any news? What are they doing to find my brother?"

"Slow down, Salome," Marlena said. "Give them a minute to get indoors. Why don't you go get everyone some iced tea?"

Iced tea? Was she crazy? I ignored Marlena and stood my ground.

The blond man extended his hand to me. "I'm Frank. This is Mick. I can answer some of your questions."

I shook his hand and stared into his face, trying in vain to be brave. I had to know the details.

"I was a witness," Frank said. "I saw the man who captured your brother. Saw his face. He grabbed Cain, tossed him into the back of a car and took off. I've provided a description of the man and the car and they're looking for him. That's all I know."

I couldn't stop myself from flying into the

arms of this friend of Cain's. "Thank you, thank you, thank you," I mumbled into his shirt between tears.

"We didn't know," Marlena said, patting my back. "We were only told he was missing. This means so much. Come in, please. Cain's parents will be home shortly. The Colonel's going to be furious he wasn't told about this."

"The Colonel?" Mick asked.

"Dad," I said, lifting my face from Frank's shirt and looking up at him. Mick was sending a questioning look Frank's way.

"He never said his dad was a Colonel," Frank said releasing me. "But he talked about his beautiful sister all the time. I was even with him when he found your birthday present. Did you like it?"

At once I was ashamed. I'd been almost afraid of the perfectly wrapped gift sitting like a sentinel on the window sill of my bedroom. I ran to get it. I brought it back to the living room where Marlena had seated the soldiers and carefully positioned the gift on the coffee table. I took a deep breath and peeled away the tape holding down the ends. I slipped the orange paper off and laid it aside. I sucked in my breath, completely taken aback by the beauty of the object inside.

An Arabic design of interlinking swirls in blue and green tiles decorated the surface of a small box. There were levels of intricacy and exotic mystery that I couldn't decipher in one examination. I wanted to secrete the box in my room where I could study it at my leisure. It was the perfect gift and Cain was the only one in the entire world who would realize what this would mean to me. He had indeed chosen it especially for me, his little puzzle protégé.

"How lovely," Marlena said. "What's inside?"

I lifted the lid and peered into the satin-lined interior. "A photo," I said and took it out. It was a picture of Cain in his fatigues with his arms around Mick and Frank, standing in front of a parked car. I showed the picture to Marlena. Her face softened and took on a dusky glow of pleasure. "I haven't seen this one," she said. "It must be recent." She touched Cain's face, and then passed the picture to Frank.

"Hey, Mick. Remember this?"

Mick took the picture and nodded. "Oh, baby, do I ever. Bagdad. We were working on the school that day."

"No, the hospital. Remember? That very

pregnant chick took the picture. You cracked a joke about her being its first customer."

"Oh, yeah, sure man. I remember now. Sensitive, wasn't she? Started yelling some gibberish."

Frank handed the picture back to me. "Yeah, well, you're just lucky Cain knew enough Arabic to smooth things over. He probably convinced her you were just stupid and not intentionally insulting."

I placed the picture on the coffee table, picked up the decorated box again, and examined the kaleidoscope patterns on the surface.

"Perfect place to hide your valuables," Marlena said.

I smiled a knowing smile. Cain's gift would hold its own secret. Nothing I could keep inside would be as valuable to me.

My parents arrived a little later. When Dad heard Frank's story, he immediately contacted Lt. Rita Parker. She promised to look into it at once. My parents insisted that Mick and Frank stay in Cain's room and they, in turn, insisted on helping grill burgers and make lemonade. During dinner, they regaled us with stories of military life and adventures with Cain.

After dinner, Marlena was bragging to the visitors about Dad's inventions and Mom's oil paintings. When she started in on how smart Cain and I were, I had trouble keeping my eyes open. I took my Arabic jewelry box with me to my room, intending to study it further for a secret chamber or something, but I just couldn't stay awake. I placed it on my night stand and fell into a dreamless sleep.

The next morning I woke to a fierce headache. I headed to the kitchen for a pain killer and coffee. Everyone else was already up and having breakfast, but I couldn't eat.

"What's wrong, honey?" Mom asked.

"I feel horrible," I muttered. "My head's pounding and my mouth's like dust. Think I'll just go back to bed 'til the aspirin takes effect."

"The boys are leaving this morning," Mom said. "Dad's taking them down to Carlton so the taxi won't have to tackle this mountain again."

I turned to Frank and Mick. "Thank you so much for your visit. It really means a lot to me."

Frank flashed his gorgeous grin. "Get well soon," he said.

"Don't thank us, kid," Mick said. "We couldn't come back to the States without Cain and not visit his family. Hopefully, when we get back over there they'll have found him and we can have a real party."

"Any word yet from Lt. Parker?" I asked Dad.

He shook his head and looked grave.

I nodded and left the room, intending to lie down. As I walked through the living room on my way back to bed I noticed the front door was slightly ajar. Someone had already been out enjoying the fresh morning air. The idea appealed to me and I stepped out onto the porch.

I breathed in the invigorating spring smells and stretched my arms over my head, beginning to feel a little more awake. I stepped off the porch and struck out across the lawn hoping to catch a glimpse of the deer that frequented the clearing behind the garage where Dad puts out salt blocks. The bottoms of my pajama pants grew heavy from the dew and my bare feet got cold, but it helped clear the cobwebs from my brain. I slowed down when I reached the back corner of the garage and peeked around. There were two does and a buck in the clearing. The buck stood stock still, peering at the woods, on guard against potential predators. The females were licking the salt block. They hadn't noticed me, so I remained as still as possible and enjoyed the view.

The sound of the garage door rolling up the metal tracks caused the three deer, and myself, to startle. The deer focused on the garage; I remained focused on them. I watched the ears of the buck flick forward toward the sound of the voices. I heard goodbye's being said and recognized sadness in Mom's voice. The buck's magnificent muscles twitched in anticipation of flight. I imagined hugs and waves and was glad no one knew I was just around the corner. Dad's truck roared to life and the deer sprang into the safety of the woods, two leaps apiece. I stayed put in the safety of my own little private corner and prayed for Cain.

When the sound of the truck's engine faded away, I continued my therapeutic stroll around the yard. By the time I found my new jewelry box shattered into pieces on the ground outside the kitchen window, my headache was gone.

Mom and Marlena appeared within seconds of my outcry. I was on my knees in the wet grass, tears gathering in my eyes, trying to reassemble the fragments. I looked up at them in confusion.

"Who did this?" I demanded. "Who would

do this?" My hands trembled with a mixture of anger and sorrow.

When Dad returned home, I was attempting to reassemble the broken box, with some success. I'd wracked my brain to understand why Frank or Mick had done this, for it had to have been one of them who crept into my room during the night. Dad's comprehension of the situation turned into his quiet form of anger, impressive and frightening.

"Salome," he said after a minute. "You woke with a headache?"

I nodded.

"Did you find a secret opening in the box?"

"Well," I said, "there is one, but I didn't find it until now. See." I showed him how the pieces fit together to conceal a chamber. "There's nothing in it. Anymore, anyway."

He thought a while longer. My Dad's an even better puzzler than Cain. He was a code breaker in the military and taught Cain our little game.

"What did Cain's secret message say?"

In retrospect, this statement should not have surprised me. Of course Dad would know of my secret messages from Cain. I'd been foolish to think otherwise. But, I just stared at him, dumbfounded, as if he'd just asked me if I was ready for the return trip to our home planet in some far off quadrant of outer space.

"Well?"

I did a mental shake. "No. I mean, I haven't looked yet."

"Go get the key." His voice was still hard. I didn't hesitate.

I retrieved the well-worn sheaf of papers, each with little spaces cut out, through which messages would appear. Fortunately, I had placed the letter from Cain in my night stand and not in the ill-fated jewelry box. I spread out Cain's correspondence on the table top. His first word, My, had two letters, so I went to page two of the code. I lay this page on top of the letter and read the words that appeared in the cut-out boxes:

Today	*I*	*watched*	*the*
exchange		*of*	*secret*
	info	*Sending*	
		you	
	something	*hidden*	
	in	*Marlena's*	*gift.*

I couldn't believe I'd forgotten all about

Marlena's package. I ran to unearth the second gift from the depths of my closet while Dad read over the decoded message. The message was whirling through my thoughts as I threw aside the clothes I'd piled on top of the old purse. What had Cain meant by the exchange of secret info? My box had held a picture of Cain standing with Frank and Mick. The picture hadn't been hidden, but what if something was hidden in the photo? What if the picture was meant to implicate Frank or Mick or both in this exchange of secret info?

Since they took the photo with them, it must be incriminating. I tried to recall the details. It was only the three of them standing along a street, in front of a car, with slightly out of focus buildings in the background. But then again, they had smashed my box, searching for something else, something Cain might have hidden in the secret chamber. If a real clue had been hidden in the secret chamber, it was now long gone.

Dad was on the phone with Lt. Rita Parker when I returned to the living room with Marlena's gift. He sounded frustrated. I didn't even give the package to Marlena, but tore off the orange wrapping paper myself. My heart beat faster when I gazed upon the gift. It was nearly identical to mine and beautiful in its perfection. I looked inside, but the silk-lined interior was empty. I felt around the surface for a catch which would reveal the secret chamber. I ran my finger ever so slowly along the edges, but I couldn't locate the trigger that would open the concealed space within the box. All the while my mind was racing with questions.

What could Cain's secret be? Why would Frank and Mick want it? It must be important for those two masqueraders to follow the package to our mountain-top home all the way from Iraq. It might be so important that it was the reason that Cain was kidnapped in the first place. Why hadn't I just solved Cain's puzzle right away? I was ready to go get the hammer and smash this box as well, when I found a nick along the edge of the center tile. I pressed it and a levered door fell open on the side of the lid.

I peered into the opening. There was something folded up and wedged in there. I used an ink pen to tease out an edge and pulled out a piece of paper that had been folded to fit the tiny space. I unfolded the paper and examined the writing on the inside. It consisted of a series of letters and numbers, KBL 417 SH, which reminded me of something I'd seen recently. I racked my brain then recalled the picture that was in my gift. The license plate on the car had a series of numbers and letters arranged similar to this. I handed the piece of paper to Dad.

"It's a license plate number," I said.

"Lt. Parker, patch me through to General Holbrook," Dad said after reading the scrap of paper. Not even Lt. Parker would ignore the tone in Dad's voice. "George," Dad said after a minute, "we've found something here you should know about." He explained the mysterious actions of our visitors, the coded message in Cain's letter, and what I'd found in the secret chamber.

Big wheels began to turn.

The next three days and nights were sheer agony. My mind wouldn't stop. My guilt wouldn't stop. If only I were as smart as Cain and didn't need to use the key I would have seen his true message right away. If only I'd been stronger, I wouldn't have crumpled, hidden the letter away, unable to participate in what I took for a childish game. Cain had been counting on me and I let him down. What if it was too late?

I froze every time the phone rang. When Mom handed the phone to Dad saying it was

General Holbrook, I held my breath. My heart pounded with fear.

"Yes, George," Dad said, then listened. I saw the stern lines on his face relax and I took a cautious breath. Then he reached out for Mom, who was standing nearby clenching a dishtowel to death, and pulled her into a hug. He broke out into a smile then kissed Mom's cheek. "They found him," he told us. "He's okay."

Marlena and I squealed. We cried, we laughed and hugged each other in joy.

When Dad hung up, he filled us in on the sketchy details they could piece together so far. The license number I had found in the jewelry box led them to a terrorist hideout where Cain was being held. Cain had accidentally witnessed a suspicious encounter between the terrorist leader and Frank. When he confronted Frank later, demanding an explanation, Frank slugged him and enlisted Mick to help transport Cain to the terrorist lair. The general didn't know yet why Cain wasn't killed outright, but Dad suspected he was going to be used in a prisoner exchange attempt.

I answered the phone when it rang a few minutes later. It was Lt. Parker. She offered her congratulations and actually started crying. I found it hard to hate her after that. Lt. Parker promised to arrange a phone call with Cain as soon as possible and also to get us on a flight to Germany to see for ourselves that he was whole and safe and alive.

Our reunion was the best. Cain had lost a lot of weight, but otherwise he was gloriously normal. He said that what kept him going was the certainty that I would find his evidence. I must have apologized a thousand times for taking so long, but he just laughed and gave me hugs.

We found out that Frank had been with him when he purchased my gift and knew of the secret chamber. But neither Mick nor Frank realized Cain went back later and bought a second gift for Marlena. When Cain accidentally saw Frank's meeting with Abdul Al-Saheb, he wrote down the car's number, hid a copy in the jewelry box and mailed them both to me.

Marlena insisted that I keep the second jewelry box as my own. She doesn't get excited about hidden chambers and secret messages. She did get excited, however, with Cain's replacement birthday present for her, an engagement ring—with no puzzle attached.

Author Bios

Here are short biographical sketches of the contributing authors, in the same order as their stories.

Terrie Farley Moran's short stories have been published in various anthologies. Her 1930's noir short, "When A Bright Star Fades," was named a Distinguished Mystery Story of 2008. Her paranormal mystery, "The Awareness," is in the recently released MWA anthology, *Crimes By Moonlight*, edited by Charlaine Harris. Terrie's ideal day includes hanging out with any or all of her seven grandchildren. A lifelong New Yorker, Terrie can be found on the web at www.womenofmystery.net

Dorothy Francis lives in Iowa, recalling 20 winters spent in the Florida Keys. The most recent books in her 'Key West Mystery' series are *Cold Case Killer* and *Eden Palms Murder*. Scheduled for 2011 is *Killer In Control*. Her most prized writing honor is her 1999 Derringer Award from the Short Mystery Fiction Society.

Dorothy resides in an independent Living Complex near her husband, Richard, a patient at the Iowa Veteran's Home.

Big Jim Williams, author of the audio books, *The Old West*, and *Tall Tales of the Old West*, has written for radio theatre, and for *Western Horseman, Livestock Weekly, Radio World, Writers' Journal, The Cardroom Poker News, Sniplits, ROPE and WIRE, WritersWeekly*, and other publications, and anthologies. A Korean War veteran and lifelong broadcaster, he writes, haunts bookstores, and naps in Goleta, CA. Married, he has two sons, four grandchildren, and welcomes emails: bigjimwilliams2@cox.net.

Elizabeth Zelvin is a New York City psychotherapist and author of *Death Will Get You Sober* and *Death Will Help You Leave Him*. The series includes two short stories nominated for the Agatha Award for Best Short Story. Liz's short stories have appeared in *Ellery Queen's Mystery Magazine* and various anthologies and webzines. She is currently working on a novel about Columbus's second voyage and a CD of her own songs titled *Outrageous Older Woman*.

Lina Zeldovich is a Russian-born New York writer and a recipient of two *Writer's Digest* Fiction Awards, the second one for an excerpt from **Death by Scheherazade's Veil**. Her latest publications include "Ultimate Comfort" in **Voices from the Garage**, and "Perfect Takedown" in **Thrills Kills n' Chills**. *Beat to a Pulp* will feature her story "Believe" in December. Her other passions are filmmaking, theater, traveling off-the-beaten-path and, of course, belly dancing!

Charles Schaeffer, a Navy veteran, lives in DC-suburban Maryland with his wife Liza, where he writes mostly short mysteries. His story, "Foul Play" appears in the **2010 Deadly Inc. Anthology**. He is back to back winner of the *Alfred Hitchcock Magazine's* "Mysterious Photo Contest". He is first place winner in Mysterical-E for "Silent Night, Deadly Night", and the Press Club's Consumer Journalism Award. He is a hobbyist wine enthusiast.

Howard B. Carron is a librarian, musician, teacher, writer, chef, ceramist, silversmith, sculptor, wood block artist, and the editor-in-chief of *Cigar Lovers Magazine*. He taught in the

Orient, the Pacific and Europe. His published stories include: "The Last Habano" in *Medley of Murder*, "A Favor for the Mayor" in *Medium of Murder*, "Christmas Came Late" in *How Not to Survive the Holidays*, and "The Old Miner" in *How NOT to Survive a Vacation*.

Brendan DuBois of New Hampshire is the award-winning author of twelve novels and more than 100 short stories. His short fiction has appeared in numerous magazines and anthologies including *The Best American Mystery Stories of the Century*, published in 2000 by Houghton-Mifflin. His short stories have twice won him the Shamus Award from the Private Eye Writers of America, and have also earned him three Edgar nominations. Visit his website at www.BrendanDuBois.com

Janis Patterson also writes romances as Janis Susan May, children's books as Janis Susan Patterson and scholarly works as J.S.M. Patterson. *Sing a Song of Spying*, a mostly fictional romantic adventure, will be released in Winter 2010, and *Danny and the Dustbunnies* in October 2010. Janis and her husband, a Naval Reserve Captain currently on overseas deployment, live in Texas with three rescued furbabies: two neurotic cats and a terribly spoiled little dog.

Barb Goffman has been nominated twice for the Agatha Award, for "The Worst Noel" in *The Gift of Murder* and "Murder at Sleuthfest" from *Chesapeake Crimes II*. Her newest published stories: "The Contest" in *Deadly Ink 2010 Short Story Collection* and "Volunteer of the Year" in *Chesapeake Crimes: They Had It Comin'*. Program chair of the Malice Domestic convention, Barb lives in Virginia with her miracle dog, Scout (a three-time cancer survivor!). www.barbgoffman.com

S. M. Harding has had over a dozen short stories published in various crime fiction publications and is currently editing *Writing Murder*, a collection of essays by Midwest authors on creating crime fiction, for Crum Creek Press. Look for "Tinkers Damn" in *Back to the Middle of Nowhere* (Pill Hill Press) and "The Hollow Hour" in *A Cup of Joe* (Wicked East Press) later this year and please visit her website at www.smharding.com

Diana Catt is married with three kids, a microbiologist and the current president of the Indiana Sisters in Crime. Her latest two publications include: a mystery, "Boneyard Busted", in *Bedlam at the Brickyard*, Blue River Press (May, 2010) and a sci-fi, "Au Naturel", in *Patented DNA*, Pill Hill Press (July, 2010). Her upcoming release: "And Through the Woods" will appear in *Back to the Middle of Nowhere: Horror in Rural America*, Pill Hill Press.

LaVergne, TN USA
22 September 2010
198056LV00001B/2/P